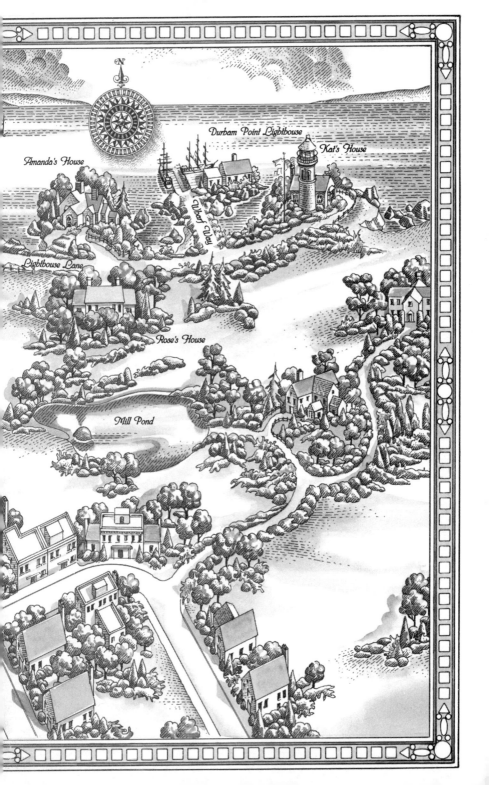

THOMAS KINKADE

The Girls of Lighthouse Lane

Katherine's Story

A CAPE LIGHT NOVEL

By Erika Tamar

HarperCollins*Publishers*

A PARACHUTE PRESS BOOK

T 9398

Library of Congress Cataloging-in-Publication Data
Katherine's story / by Thomas Kinkade and Erika Tamar. — 1st ed.
    p. cm. — (The girls of Lighthouse Lane ; #1)
    "A Parachute Press Book."
    Summary: In 1905, while pursuing her dreams of becoming an artist, the twelve-
year-old daughter of the Cape Light lighthouse keeper learns the value of family, home,
and friendship.
    ISBN 0-06-054341-8 — ISBN 0-06-054342-6 (lib. bdg.)
    [1. Artists — Fiction. 2. Lighthouses — Fiction. 3. Family life — New England —
Fiction. 4. New England — History — Fiction.] I. Tamar, Erika. II. Title.
PZ7.K6192Kat 2004   2003009555
[Fic] — dc21   CIP
                                                      AC

1 2 3 4 5 6 7 8 9 10
❖
First Edition

The Girls of Lighthouse Lane

Katherine's Story

⊱ *one* ⊰

Katherine Williams ran across the village green in the center of Cape Light at breakneck speed. Her auburn braids flew behind her as she pulled her friend Amanda Morgan along.

"Wait, Kat!" Amanda gasped. "We're supposed to walk like ladies."

"I can't wait another minute!" Kat said. Her schoolbooks, held together by a leather strap, swung in wide arcs, bumping her leg as she streaked over the grass. "They said it would take two weeks and it's way past that!"

Kat had rushed to the general store/post office every single day after school and she didn't care at all if Mr. Thomas, the postmaster, rolled his eyes when she came in again. It was already Friday, October thirteenth. How much longer could the mail take? "My package just has to be in today!"

All week long—after the usual God bless Mother,

Father, my brothers James and Todd, and all the ships at sea—her prayers had ended with "and please give me *patience.*"

But she was all out of patience. Her long skirt whirled around her ankles as she tugged at Amanda.

"All right, I'm coming." Amanda laughed, and they ran across the green to the cobblestones of East Street.

The brilliant fall colors of the oaks and maples surrounding the square passed by in a blur. Kat caught the scent of cinnamon doughnuts as she rushed by the bakery. The slow and steady *clop-clop* of the iceman's horse and the squeak of his wagon rang out from over on North Street.

"Oops." Kat almost ran into a little boy who stood in her way. He had one arm firmly wrapped around the red-and-white pole in front of the barbershop, to keep his momma from pulling him through the door. Her little brother James would do the very same thing and Ma would get so mad! Kat would have slowed down to see the boy and his momma tussle, but not today—not when the postmaster might have her package *right now*!

Two elderly sisters walking arm in arm under a parasol stopped and frowned. "Isn't that the Williams girl galloping by?" one said. "And with the minister's daughter!" the other finished.

Kat and Amanda skidded to a stop in front of the general store's glass door. The bell rang when they opened the door, but Mr. Thomas barely looked up. He was busy talking to some men gathered in front of the potbellied stove.

"Well, I say Teddy Roosevelt will go down in history as one of the great presidents. You can't deny that 1905 has been a year of peace, progress, and prosperity."

"No one thought much of Teddy when he was McKinley's vice president. If it wasn't for McKinley's assassination . . . "

"Imagine, six children in the White House! And all those animals—dogs, rabbits, badgers, even a small black bear!"

"It sure keeps things lively down there in Washington, D.C."

Kat and Amanda stood at the counter and waited. Kat caught the aromas from the pickle barrel and the wheel of cheddar mixed with the fragrance of coffee beans. The counter was piled high with bolts of fabric. Behind it, there were cubbyholes for mail. Kat got up on her toes and leaned far over the counter. She knew Mr. Thomas kept packages on the floor behind it, but she couldn't see any.

Kat tapped her foot.

"I hear Joe Hardy over at the telegraph office got word of a storm traveling up the coast from Hatteras."

Now they were starting a whole *new* conversation! Kat knew she must not interrupt grown-ups, but she was badly tempted.

"Might veer off to sea before it ever reaches us here in New England," Mr. Thomas said over his shoulder as he finally ambled toward Kat and Amanda. "Afternoon, girls. Suppose you're looking for your package again, Katherine?"

"Yes, Mr. Thomas," Kat said. "Did it come? Did it?"

"Well, something came for Miss Katherine Williams, but it's not what you've been waiting for." He bent down to rummage under the counter.

"It's not?" Kat asked.

"Didn't you say you were expecting paint? I guess your father's repainting the lighthouse daymark." He put a narrow package wrapped in brown paper on the counter. "Well, there are no cans of paint in this. Too small and flat."

"It's not for my father, Mr. Thomas." Anyone could see the daymark didn't need repainting! The bright red and yellow stripes painted on the side made the light-house a clearly visible daytime landmark for sailors. "It's

4

for *me*." Kat beamed as she grabbed the package. "Four tubes of watercolor paints." She had convinced Papa to give her birthday money in advance—well, only three months, not *that* far ahead—so she could order the paints from an art supply catalog. "Thank you, Mr. Thomas!"

Kat started to rip open the brown wrapping paper. Then she stopped herself. She couldn't bear the thought of one of the tubes falling out and getting lost on the way home.

Kat hugged the package close to her heart as she and Amanda left the store. A few steps along East Street brought them to Lighthouse Lane, the longest road in Cape Light. It ran the entire length of the town all the way to the lighthouse at Durham Point where Kat lived.

"Burnt sienna, cerulean blue! Don't they sound luscious?" Kat said. "Alizarin crimson! Cobalt violet!"

This part of Lighthouse Lane, next to the green, was paved and it had the fanciest houses. Kat's cousin Lizabeth lived in one of the largest homes. Kat glanced at its porch, picket fence, and rose-covered trellis as they passed.

"You paint beautifully with the colors you already have," Amanda said.

"Well, I've been mixing the colors to make new

ones, but I can't always get them right. Now it will be so much easier."

Tall trees arched overhead. Kat studied the turning leaves. Definitely sienna and crimson and a touch of gold, she thought. Oh, she couldn't wait to dip her paintbrush into the new colors! A little voice inside her was singing, "so happy, so happy," and she couldn't help skipping.

"If I keep trying, if I learn more . . . I want to be a real artist someday!"

"Miss Cotter always hangs your pictures in the classroom. And you're the one she picks to help the little kids with drawing," Amanda said. "Everyone in school knows you're the best at art. Doesn't that satisfy you?"

"No! I'm talking about being a *serious* artist. In a big city, where things *happen*. I'd paint and never even think of all my lighthouse chores. I'm so tired of them! I'd go to the great museums and look at the masterpieces close up. I've only seen pictures of them in books and that's not the same at all. And there'd be bright lights and crowds of interesting people doing exciting things and trolley cars—I'd ride a trolley every day!"

They skipped along Lighthouse Lane until it turned

into a dirt road and curved toward the ocean. Kat liked the whalebone decorations on the some of the lawns.

"You wouldn't really leave Cape Light, would you?" Amanda asked.

"I really would. There's never anything new here. Do you know there are *moving stairs* that take you from floor to floor at the R.H. White store in Boston? I want to see that!"

They were almost at Amanda's cottage nestled among tall trees, overlooking the shore. Kat could hear the waves crashing against the rocks below the parsonage.

"Less than half a mile left to go," Kat said. Amanda's house was about halfway between the village green and Kat's home.

"I'm glad that Hannah is playing at Mary Margaret's house this afternoon." Amanda smiled. "I feel as free as anything, without a single thing to do until dinner! I'm not even going to drop off my schoolbooks. I can't wait to get to the lighthouse."

I shouldn't complain about the lighthouse chores, Kat thought. It's so much harder for Amanda to take care of her little sister, Hannah, and keep house for her father.

Amanda glanced at the house opposite the parsonage as they passed by. "Kat, there *is* something new in

Cape Light. You know old Mr. Reynolds, across the lane from me?"

"Yes."

"He's moving out to live with his daughter and her family in Cranberry. So a new family will be moving in."

"Do you know who they are?"

"No. But Father says the house is already sold," Amanda said.

They came to the steep hill where Lighthouse Lane led down to the shore and the docks. In the winter, it was famous as the best sledding hill in Cape Light.

Kat ran down the hill, skidding on pebbles, trying to slide part of the way. *"Whee!"*

Amanda followed more cautiously.

Leaves had drifted down and collected in huge piles at the bottom. Suddenly, Kat whirled around and dove into one.

"Kat!"

"Come on, Amanda!"

Amanda hesitated. "We're not children anymore. We can't be jumping in leaves. I'm *thirteen*."

Kat grinned up at Amanda. "Well, I'm only twelve and three-quarters, so I guess I'm still allowed to have fun."

"Your petticoat is showing! If anyone sees us . . ."

"No one's here but us." Kat grabbed a handful of leaves and tossed it at Amanda. "And I'll never tell."

Amanda looked all around—then jumped in. Kat laughed—she knew Amanda couldn't resist! They jumped from pile to pile, laughing and sliding.

"Got you!" Amanda shouted as she showered Kat with a handful of leaves.

"Got you back!" One of Kat's braids unraveled; the loose hair streamed down her back and tangled with twigs. It blended perfectly with the red and russet leaves.

Kat suddenly stopped. "Oh, no!"

"What? What's wrong?" Amanda asked.

"I forgot! Aunt Sue and Lizabeth are coming over and Ma asked me to tidy up. You know how *perfect* my cousin is, and Aunt Sue will look me over and criticize. Let's brush this stuff off and get going!"

Amanda quickly brushed herself off, but bits of leaves, twigs, and dirt stuck to Kat's rough wool skirt. Kat worked furiously to pick it all off.

Amanda turned back toward the hill. "Kat, I think I hear a horse and carriage."

"It can't be them, not yet! Quick, help me braid my hair. What happened to my ribbon?"

"Too late," Amanda said. "It's them! Coming over

the top of the hill!"

"Oh, no! I'll hide! I'll hide until they pass!"

Kat dove into a pile of leaves before she finished her sentence and buried herself. Just in time, she thought. She could hear the horse's hooves coming closer.

Crumbled leaves tickled Kat's face. The carriage wheels squeaked. They sounded louder and louder, closer and closer. The carriage had to be very near now. She couldn't see a thing. Her nose itched. She was going to sneeze! She couldn't, she just couldn't! She pressed her finger against her upper lip—that helped a little. How long could it take for them to pass by? Please, *giddyap*!

Suddenly, Kat heard Aunt Sue say "Whoa!" The sound of the horse's hooves stopped. One last squeal from the wheels—right next to her! Then silence. What was happening?

"Hi, Amanda." It was Lizabeth's voice. "Are you going over to Kat's? We'll give you a ride."

"Thank you," said Amanda.

Oh, good, Kat thought. I'll catch up with them later.

"Oh, dear!" Aunt Sue's voice rang out. "Over there. Is that a leg? Is that a human leg?"

"Where, mother?" Lizabeth asked.

"Where? Where?" her four-year-old sister Tracy echoed.

"Yes, it is! A leg—a human leg—sticking out of that pile of leaves!"

Kat's face turned hot. She was caught!

"A woman's leg, bare to the knee!" Aunt Sue said. "Oh, dear! We need to get help! We need to get someone!"

Kat lay still in absolute panic. What should she do now?

"Don't look, children." Aunt Sue's voice was shaky. "It could be a dead body!"

And then Kat heard Lizabeth say, "I think . . . I think I'm going to swoon!"

❧ *two* ❧

Kat scrunched under the leaves and wished she could disappear. She had to do *something* before Aunt Sue went for help! She didn't have a whole lot of choices.

Kat jumped out of the leaves, shedding a trail of debris.

Aunt Sue's mouth formed an O, exactly like a surprised cartoon character in the Sunday funnies. If Kat hadn't been so embarrassed, she might have laughed.

"Katherine Williams!" Aunt Sue wore a large toque with a satin band on top of her high-piled hair. The hat bobbed as she spoke.

"Good afternoon, Aunt Sue," Katherine said weakly. She knew her face was bright red. She smoothed her skirt down to her ankles.

"What in the world were you doing?" Aunt Sue asked. Lizabeth and Tracy stared.

Kat swallowed. "Just . . . playing."

"What are you playing?" Tracy piped up. "Can I play?"

"Not now," Kat mumbled.

As usual, Kat thought, Lizabeth's long, wavy golden hair looked perfect. Today it was held back with a lavender ribbon to match her silky lavender dress. The dress had puffy shoulders and tight long sleeves and ended with a lavender-and-pale-blue-striped ruffle at her ankles. She had worn the exact same dress to school that day and it was still wrinkle-free and spotless. How did she do it? A soft, pale blue shawl was draped perfectly over her shoulders and her ankle-high patent leather boots were polished enough to really shine. Even Tracy, a smaller version of twelve-year-old Lizabeth, was unnaturally neat for a four-year-old.

Lizabeth's eyes swept over Kat, from her messy head to her wrinkled skirt down to her dusty shoes.

"Katherine—" Aunt Sue shook her head. "Never mind. Get into the carriage, girls."

Kat tried to brush herself off. Awkwardly, she picked up her schoolbooks and her package. Well, at least her cousin Christopher wasn't with them today; he was fourteen and a champion at wisecracks.

Kat glanced at Amanda. She looked as if she was

holding back a giggle. That made Kat's mouth twitch, too. They squeezed into the back of the carriage next to Tracy.

Aunt Sue adjusted the reins and the carriage moved forward. Beyond the hill, Lighthouse Lane curved toward the rocky shore and ran alongside the ocean. Kat kept her eyes on the passing scenery. She knew if she looked at Amanda she'd have a fit of giggles.

There were few houses here and the lane was lined by dense brush, beach plum, and sea grass. They passed by Wharf Way and the busy docks. White sails bobbed in the distance and the smell of fish drifted into the carriage. Then they passed the bait and tackle shed and the rowboat rental sign.

"Your face is dirty," Tracy told Kat.

They passed Alveira & Sons Boatyard. Kat smelled fresh-cut wood and shellac.

Lizabeth turned toward Kat. "What *were* you doing? Honestly!"

"Nothing!" Sometimes her cousin could be so irritating! "Anyway, what was all that about swooning?"

"I don't know." Lizabeth laughed. "I read it in a book. I've never *swooned* in my life."

Kat couldn't help smiling. Just when she was most annoyed with Lizabeth for putting on airs, her cousin could suddenly become real and laugh at herself. By the time they reached the lighthouse and the cottage at Durham Point, Kat, Amanda, and Lizabeth were all laughing together.

They piled into the cottage. While everyone exchanged greetings, Kat's big white dog, part husky and part mystery, barked and ran in welcoming circles around her. "Hi, Sunshine!"

"Jamie! Jamie!" Tracy made a dash for Kat's little brother James. For some strange reason she adored him, and James was as tolerant of her as an eight-year-old could be. Todd, at ten, kept a careful distance.

"Tracy, don't *hug!*" James pleaded. "I'll play with you only if you don't *hug.*"

All of them were crowded in the combination living room/dining room/kitchen. A short hall led to Ma and Papa's bedroom. Kat's tiny room was upstairs next to her brothers', tucked under the attic eaves.

It was so different from Lizabeth's house, where there was a separate room for every single thing, even a parlor that the grown-ups used only on special occasions and the children weren't allowed to enter. The parlor had shining parquet wood floors, a grandfather clock, a tufted crimson velvet couch, and a big potted palm.

What was the sense of a room that was just for show, Kat wondered. Anyway, she had the lighthouse tower—it was her special haven where she felt completely at ease. And it had a *round* room, surely the only one in town.

Ma was wrestling the laundry through the wringer in the big kitchen sink. Her feet were firmly braced against the stone floor and Kat could see the strain in her back as she worked. "I'm just about done. I'll hang it up to dry later. There's coffee on. And Kat, please get the muffins out of the oven." Ma dried her hands on her apron and embraced Aunt Sue.

They looked alike, with the same ash-blond hair. Aunt Sue was five years older, Kat knew, but she looked younger. Ma's hands were rough and chapped; Aunt Sue's hands were soft, white, and sparkling with jewels.

Kat was careful at the wood-burning stove; sometimes an ember sparked up suddenly. She popped muffins out of the baking tin and put them on a big blue-and-white enameled plate. "Where's Papa?"

"At the docks helping to tie down the boats. They say there's a squall coming in by morning." Ma raised her eyebrows. "You could rebraid your hair, Kat."

Kat shrugged. What was the point? It was certainly too late to impress Aunt Sue.

Hard work had lined Ma's face, but Aunt Sue had the pampered look of a banker's wife with lots of servants. Two sisters, starting off together—it wasn't fair! Papa had once been the captain of his own whaler. But the ship had been lost in an accident at sea, an accident that injured Pa's leg and kept him from working on the slippery deck of a boat. He had a bad limp when he was tired. He tried to hide it but Kate noticed. She felt a special closeness to Papa and she wouldn't trade him for anyone, but she wished Ma had an easier life.

"Come on, let's go to the lighthouse," Lizabeth said.

That's where they always went as soon as Lizabeth and Amanda arrived at Durham Point. Up in the tower room it seemed as if the rest of the world, with all its rules and judgments, fell away. That's where a peaceful stillness came over Kat. That's where she painted and felt most free to dream.

Ma put some muffins on a separate plate. "Here, take them up with you."

Amanda held the muffin plate and Kat carried her package and a jar of water. She was going to paint today for sure!

They rushed to the lighthouse. Even Lizabeth forgot about taking dainty steps, Kat thought. They hurried up the three wide stone stairs at the base and then climbed the ladder going straight up the dimly lit stone shaft. At the top of the ladder, the sunlight suddenly streaming into the tower room was dazzling.

The small round room, just under the second ladder to the light itself, was their special place. There was just enough space for a few high-back chairs, a low three-legged table, a faded rag rug to warm the stone floor, and a coal-burning stove. Deep windowsill shelves held supplies: a kerosene lantern, a sack of coal, some of Papa's tools, packets of wire and cord, rags and cleanser, a few dog-eared books, and Kat's art supplies.

The room was plain as could be, but the big windows curving all around made it extraordinary. The ocean below stretched as far as she could see. Waves crashed with furious sprays of white foam on the strip of sandy beach. Huge rocks, some half-hidden in the water and some jagged on shore, were as shiny-wet and black as seals. Kat gazed out at miles and miles of sky. This is how it must look from the very top of the world, she thought.

"It's so beautiful," Lizabeth breathed.

"Every time I come here, it feels sort of like I'm coming home," Amanda said.

"Me, too," Lizabeth said. Then she giggled. "If

lighthouses could talk, this one would be saying 'Welcome back, girls,' and 'Come on in.'"

Amanda flopped down cross-legged on the rag rug. "Want to play jacks? I bet I can get up to sevensies."

"Not today," Kat said. "I want to try my new colors."

Lizabeth perched on a chair near the stove. "Let's just talk; it's so nice without brothers and sisters around. Tracy is such a pest!"

"I think she's sweet," Amanda said.

"That's because you don't have to live with her. She gets into all my things. I need a lock on my door. And then there's Christopher. He teases me too much!"

"Well, that's what big brothers do," Kat said. Her cousin Chris was pretty nice and some of Lizabeth's prissy ways almost begged for teasing.

Lizabeth shrugged and nibbled at a muffin. "Mmmm. I love cornbread."

Kat pulled the little table next to her chair and arranged her supplies on it, sniffing at her new tubes when she opened them. She loved that distinctive paint smell. She squeezed spots of paint onto the old plate she used as a palette.

"I'm almost finished with *Jane Eyre*," Lizabeth said. "Who wants it next?"

"I'll take it after Amanda," Kat said. "I want to do nothing but art this week."

"Anyway, I'm a fast reader," Amanda said.

"You'll love it. There's an orphan—that's Jane—and she becomes a governess for Rochester—he's mean and grumpy but she falls in love with him and then he—"

"Stop, don't tell us the whole story!" Amanda said.

"Oops, sorry."

Sometimes Lizabeth is so nice, Kat thought. She buys all the books she wants at the Pelican Street Bookshop and then she gives them to Amanda and me as soon as she's finished.

"Well, I'm not going to read it *twice*," she'd say whenever Kat tried to thank her for a book. "I already know what happens."

"There's a big public library in Boston." Kat gathered some paint-covered rags. "You can borrow books for free, whatever you want. Oh, I'd love to go there!"

"Why bother?" Lizabeth asked. "We have the bookshop right here and they'll order for you if the book isn't in the store. Anyway, who wants a book that's been handled by *strangers*? Maybe someone who just wiped his nose! Yuck!"

Kat dipped a brush in the jar of water and gave it a

little shake. It came to a nice, satisfying point. "Amanda, let me paint your portrait."

"Do I have to sit still? I hate that."

"You can still talk." Kat balanced her block of watercolor paper on her knees. It was thick and solid enough to support her brushstrokes, but what she wouldn't give for an easel!

"Come on, Amanda, I need a model to practice on. Please, please."

"All right." Amanda settled into a chair.

"Turn your head to the side just a little. Don't move."

Kat studied Amanda as she mixed the colors. Amanda's shoulder-length hair was light brown but there were many shades mixed in—bits of gold shining in the brown. And maybe violet highlights?

Most people would notice Lizabeth first, Kat thought. She had elegant clothes and blond hair, blue eyes and rosy cheeks. But Amanda was beautiful; pale skin, hazel eyes, a straight classic nose, a soft, gentle mouth. It took a second look to see her quiet beauty.

"I keep wondering who's going to live in the Reynolds house," Amanda said.

"They'll have to go to my father's bank for a mortgage," Lizabeth said. "So I'll find out."

"Then that's your mission for this week," Amanda said.

"I hope it's a family with children," Kat said. "It would be nice to see some new faces in school for a change."

"A lot of summer people are buying cottages down the coast in Shorehaven," Amanda said. "Maybe Cape Light will get some vacationers, too."

"We could meet interesting people from big cities," Kat said.

Lizabeth shook her head. "No, they won't come to Cape Light. Father says our shoreline is much too rocky. We only have that little strip of beach down below, hardly big enough for one boat to come in. That's not what summer people want."

"Then they don't know what they're missing," Amanda said. "Cape Light is beautiful!"

"Amanda, stop moving! You're changing the shadows!"

"I hate being your model," Amanda said. "You get so bossy."

"Sorry. It's just, well, it's confusing when the shadows on your face shift." Kat had captured Amanda's nose pretty well, but the eyes were all wrong. She had to clear her mind and concentrate on light and dark. Paint what you actually *see*, not what you *think* something looks like, she told herself.

"My neck hurts," Amanda complained.

"One more minute," Kat begged. "Please."

"Let Kat finish." Lizabeth got up for another muffin. "I want to see how it turns out."

Amanda's eyes could change from gray to gray-green in a minute. Kat couldn't get the expression right. She thought she saw sadness in them, even when Amanda was smiling. Six years was a long time to mourn, but maybe when it was your mother, the sadness never went away. Amanda's mother had died in child-birth with Hannah.

Kat remembered when Amanda, who was only seven, came back to school afterward. Everyone rushed to her to say sympathetic things. Amanda looked cornered. Kat could see she was trying not to cry. Kat went to her and took her hand without a word. Amanda gripped hers very tightly and they didn't let go for a long time.

"Kat, I have to move!"

"Just one more second. I promise."

Kat tilted her head back and squinted at the paper. The eyes didn't look anything like Amanda's. She added small flecks of green and a dab of pale yellow to catch the light. Hopeless. They were still flat and expression-less. There were no do-overs with watercolors. This was too hard! But Kat loved the way the white of the paper showed through the translucent colors, the way a spray of water could soften the outlines and get interesting effects—if she was lucky. She didn't know enough. Her little instruction book was too limited. If only she could get some real training.

Kat sighed. "All right, you can move. It doesn't matter."

Amanda stretched. "Let me see."

"No, it's awful." Kat crumpled the paper before Amanda and Lizabeth could look over her shoulder.

Lizabeth picked up some of Kat's old paintings on the shelf. "Why do you paint the same thing over and over again?" she asked.

"You mean the seascapes? Because I'm trying to get it right. Anyway, the sea is *never* the same. It's always changing. Green or black or blue. Peaceful or churning and angry. Tides reaching for the moon. . . ." She gazed out of the window. A tremendous feeling that she couldn't name swept through her. If only she could get it on paper! "Sometimes I feel—I feel as if this is almost a holy place. Even more than church."

Lizabeth nodded.

"I know," Amanda said. "I do love church, though," she quickly added.

"Your father's sermons are always good. I wasn't saying anything about that." Kat grinned. "But *I* know why you love church so much lately."

Amanda looked down at her hands. "There's no special reason."

"What about that boy who's always staring at you?" Kat teased.

"I don't know that he's looking at *me*," Amanda said. "He might be looking at someone in the row behind me."

"I've noticed, too," Lizabeth said. "His head swivels when you go up to sing with the choir."

"And don't think I haven't seen you sneaking looks at him," Kat added.

"I don't know him to talk to, but—don't you think he looks like a nice person?" Amanda blushed. "I do think he's wonderfully handsome."

"Amanda, he's nobody. I bet he's just a deckhand," Lizabeth said. "Probably came to town to work at the docks."

"How do you know? You don't know him at all!" Amanda said.

"That Sunday suit he wears to church? It has shiny worn spots," Lizabeth said.

Kat wished her cousin's snobbishness wouldn't keep slipping out.

"So what?" Amanda's eyes were fiery. "He's still handsome!"

"He must have quit school already. That's why we don't know him," Lizabeth said.

Lots of their classmates quit by age fourteen. Especially the girls. The high school for all the surrounding towns was in Cranberry; there weren't enough continuing students in any one town to fill a high school. Todd would go on for sure—maybe even to college! Papa wanted Kat to have more schooling too, even though she was a girl. Maybe it was Papa's unusual attitude that gave her the courage to dream of something more than being married at sixteen.

"I'd discourage him if I were you," Lizabeth continued.

"You're not me!" Amanda snapped.

Kat was surprised to see even-tempered Amanda flare up. She had to be really sweet on that boy, whose name they didn't even know.

"Well, *I'm* going to marry someone very rich and important," Lizabeth said.

"I believe in marrying for love," Amanda said.

"So do I, but you can decide who to love," Lizabeth said. "A woman has that one chance to have a good life. You want a man who can take care of you, don't you?"

"I don't need anyone to take care of me," Kat said. "I'm going to make my own good life. I'm going to *do* things and go places and when I'm a famous artist, I'll fall in love with someone different and exciting. Someone I'll meet in a great city." She half-closed her eyes. She could almost see it, discussing techniques with other artists in cafes, one of her paintings in a Boston gallery . . .

"Only men are famous artists," Lizabeth said.

"That's not so!" Kat protested.

"Then go ahead, name a famous woman artist," Lizabeth challenged.

"I will!" Kat's mind raced through all the artists she'd ever heard of. Sargent. Whistler. Rembrandt. . . . Not one woman's name came to her. Not *one*!

"I'll think of someone later," Kat mumbled.

Maybe Lizabeth was right. Kat's shoulders drooped. And maybe she was only good enough to be the star artist of a one-room school because she'd managed to draw good Easter bunnies in kindergarten. And judging by the way she'd botched Amanda's portrait. . . . Maybe my dreams are just hopeless, Kat thought. Is there really any way I can make them come true?

❦ *three* ❦

K at watched her brothers grab apples for dessert. They were rushing to their room to work on the telephone they were making out of baking powder boxes, drawing paper, and string. "It says how to do it in the *Handy Book*," Todd insisted. So far, their telephone didn't work at all. But the *Handy Book* was usually good; Todd had made a nifty war kite following its instructions.

Kat couldn't understand how a *real* telephone worked, much less one made out of boxes. Cranberry already had telephones and switchboard operators called hello girls. The mayor promised that telephone lines would come to Cape Light soon. Wouldn't that be wonderful! Her friend Laurel in Cranberry said her house telephone had two short rings and one long. There were eight parties on a line and you weren't supposed to pick up unless the call was for you, but Laurel listened in anyway. She said it was so funny sometimes.

"Todd, did you clean the glass around the light?" Kat called as he was about to disappear into his room.

"Yes!"

Sunshine curled under the table, with his head resting on Kat's feet. Kat moved her spoon around the last of her chowder. At the end of the month, when money was tight, it was chowder for dinner every night. James and Todd would go clamming at the rocks and come back with a good haul. Sometimes Ma made it with potatoes and milk, sometimes with tomatoes and parsley. She tried every which way to vary it, but it was still chowder and Kat was tired of it.

Ma was at the sink scrubbing the pots. "It's almost time for your watch."

"It's still daylight," Kat said, though she knew darkness could sweep over Durham Point almost without warning. She had the first watch at the lighthouse, from twilight to ten. Papa had the long night watch, then Ma took over for the early morning hours until dawn. "Ma, come sit for a minute."

"Your father will be back soon. I should reheat—oh, I guess that can wait till he gets here. I do want to just *sit*."

Ma smiled, dried her hands with the dishtowel

draped on her shoulder, and sank into a chair across from Kat. "Sorry about dessert. I didn't have time to bake a pie, with Sue visiting this afternoon. I'll make one tomorrow."

"That's all right, I like apples plain." Kat took one from the bowl in the center of the table and bit into it with a crunch. "Ma . . . whenever I see Aunt Sue . . ."

"She looks wonderful, doesn't she? And Tracy— she's growing so fast, the picture of health with those cute rosy cheeks. She's such a bright little girl." Ma laughed. "Though she does bedevil our James."

A log toppled in the fireplace and made a shower of sparks.

"I was thinking . . . about you and Aunt Sue. Ma— are you ever sorry? I mean, about being stuck in a lighthouse."

"I'm not *stuck*! I can't imagine a more wonderful place than Durham Point!"

"I know, I love it too, but—" Kat turned the apple around and around in her hand. "You work so hard and there's no *end* to it. Ma, didn't you have dreams?"

"Of course. Everyone does, Kat. Do you want to know what my dream was when I was your age?"

"Tell me, Ma."

"Well, I was just fourteen when I first saw him. I

thought Tom Williams was the best-looking, strongest, wisest . . . He had such a smile! He still does, doesn't he?"

Kat nodded. Papa could light up a room.

"Anyway, he was courting someone. That just about broke my heart. I was so young. He'd say hello to me and maybe tousle my hair—you know how your father is, friendly to everyone. But I had the impossible dream that someday, somehow, he would really *notice* me. Well, that dream came true! Of course, I helped it along by being underfoot almost any place he went."

Kat couldn't imagine that. Ma was so proper.

"It was a terrible time for us when your father lost his boat. And it's painful to see how much he still misses going to sea. But think of the women in Cape Light whose men have been taken by the sea forever. And the children lost to pneumonia and influenza and scarlet fever. I have blessing upon blessing."

"I know, but—"

"I don't love getting out of a warm, cozy bed for the morning watch—but I'm happy, Kat. I like making a home, I like puttering in the vegetable garden, I like tending the chickens."

Ma couldn't mean that. The chicken coop behind the cottage smelled!

"Ma, I want so much more! I want to live in a big city. I want my art to be *important*, not just a girlish hobby."

"I think times are changing for women, Kat. Honestly, I don't know if that's good or bad. But you can't forget to enjoy what you already have. Perhaps you could pray for contentment." Ma got up to wipe the table. "It'll be easier for you when you have more free time. Todd will be old enough to take a watch in another year or so."

"I think he's old enough right now," Kat said.

"Todd's the serious one in this family, our scholar," Mom said. "I know that makes him seem older, but he's only ten."

James still had that round, baby face and soft blond hair, Kat thought. But Todd had become tall and lean, with high cheekbones. He still wore knickers and he had that funny cowlick in his dark brown hair, but he'd lost a lot of his boyishness. Why couldn't Ma see he was growing up? It would be nice to have a few evenings off. "I still think he—"

Suddenly Sunshine jumped up and ran to the door. It burst open with a blast of cold and the smell of the sea. Papa's tall rugged shape filled the doorframe.

"Papa!"

He closed the door against the wind, pulled Ma into a bear hug, and leaned down to plant a kiss on Kat's nose. "The best freckle, second from the right," he said. "How's my favorite daughter?"

"I'm your *only* daughter!"

"If I had ten more, you'd still be my favorite!"

They'd said the exact same lines to each other since she couldn't remember when, but Kat still liked it.

"You've had a long day," Ma said.

"We got every boat tied down, every line secured, prepared for anything." Papa scratched behind Sunshine's ears. "I'm bone tired and ready for some hot chowder! Without tomatoes, I hope?"

"You have no imagination," Ma said. "There's life beyond milk and potatoes."

"Not for clams." His eyes squinted with his smile. Papa pulled off his knit wool cap. His auburn hair, the same color as Kat's, tumbled down his forehead. "So they were saying a squall by morning, but the wind feels like it's picking up. My guess is it will hit earlier. We'll lock down the shutters tonight."

"God willing, it'll pass by Cape Light," Ma said.

"And all that work for nothing?"

Kat didn't want to notice how bad Papa's limp was tonight. He sat down to pull off his work boots. "Kat, it's time to stand watch."

"I know."

"It should be a quiet night," he said. "Only a fool would take a boat out with a storm heading this way."

Kat got up reluctantly and took her yellow oilcloth slicker from the hook by the door. She hated to leave the warm circle of firelight, the smell of wood ashes, the scent of baking muffins that still hung in the air. She smiled at Sunshine curled under the table again, this time with his head resting on Papa's feet.

"I'll be up to relieve you at ten," Papa said.

He looked so tired tonight and he'd be able to snatch no more than a few hours of sleep. "You can make it later," Kat said. "Tomorrow is Saturday—no school."

Kat braced herself against the wind as she opened the door. At the base of the lighthouse, it whipped her hair around and into her face. But it wasn't hurricane force. The last time they'd had a hurricane, the outhouse tipped over and wasn't that a mess!

Clouds streaked across a darkening sky. The red and yellow daymark above her stood out in the last bit of daylight. Soon it would become invisible in the night.

Kat climbed up the lighthouse ladder to the tower room, and continued up the second ladder high into the very top to the cramped space where the light was. There was a bell in case she needed to call for help. She checked the glass around the light. Clean and clear. Todd had done a good job.

She wound the spring that made the light revolve. There was hardly room to turn around up here; her elbows bumped the stone walls. She switched on the newly electrified light and watched it turn. Its rays could be seen for miles in all directions.

Kat climbed down the ladder to the room below. They'd had an Indian summer, but the nights were cold. Ma always cleaned the ashes out of the coal stove at the end of her morning watch. It was Kat's job to stoke the new coals and keep the room warm for the long night ahead. She shoveled the coals around with an iron poker and tried to keep her hands clean.

Kat took the kerosene lantern from the shelf. She had to wash and polish the globe once a week, fill it with kerosene, and trim the wick. Well, it looked clean enough and it was full; she'd just filled it on her last shift. She trimmed the wick and lit it. The light was reflected in the dark windows.

She sat in her chair at the window facing the sea. There was nothing left to do but scan the horizon and be alert for a boat in trouble. If the fog rolled in, she would sound the fog horn.

The wind was whistling past and the ocean was choppy. She could barely see the outlines of the rocks. Everything appeared in different shades of black and gray, with no moon at all. Could she do something interesting with that? Daylight was fading too fast to think about painting. The light from the lantern was good enough for doing her arithmetic and spelling exercises, but there was no school tomorrow, so she certainly wasn't about to do homework now!

Kat looked down at the cottage. The shutters were closed. Thin lines of light escaped between the slats.

The sky had become dark. The ocean had turned pure black. Kat could no longer tell the waves from the rocks, except when the lighthouse rays swept by in their steady circle.

She wished Amanda could have stayed to sleep over; they could be sitting here together and talking quietly, just the two of them. But Amanda had too many responsibilities. "I have to pick up Hannah at Mary Margaret's and sort the clothes. The laundress is coming tomorrow," she'd said when she left this afternoon.

Kat's thoughts were interrupted by the sudden absence of sound. The normal background noises were gone. The wind had stopped. She no longer heard waves crashing against the rocks. The air felt heavy in the silence.

Kat got up and went to the window. The ocean was still, waiting. . . . It felt as though the world was holding its breath. This was it, Kat thought. The calm before the storm.

A few raindrops pattered on the glass. Then more ran down in steady streams.

Soon the patter became a thousand drums as rain pelted against the windows. Huge waves battered the shore, smashing and roaring with unleashed fury. It was magnificent. A jagged line of lightning split through the dark.

Inside, Kat felt snug and secure. Papa was always caulking and keeping on top of repairs. The lighthouse was shipshape.

She looked toward the cottage. It was completely dark. Everyone must be tucked into bed and fast asleep by now. Too bad Todd and James were missing this. They'd love the drama of the storm.

Kat turned back to the raging sea. In the lighthouse ray, she caught a glimpse of something. Was it white? Could it be a sail? No, not in the middle of a storm like this!

Kat jumped from her chair and waited for the light to sweep around again. Yes, it was a boat! Her shoulders tensed. It was tossing on the waves like a child's toy. On her watch! This wasn't a night to be out. What should she do? What *could* she do? She watched helplessly as the boat kept heading her way, making for land. Please, whoever is on that boat, let them be good sailors!

The light turned in its rhythmic circle, pinpointing the treacherous rocks. Please, let the light show them the hazards and guide them safely to the beach. The boat looked so fragile! Kat gasped. For a horrible moment, she lost sight of it behind the raging waves. No, thank God, there was the white sail again. It was coming closer on a steady course. Close enough to clearly see the beach each time the light turned. They could make it, they *had* to make it. . . .

Was that a flicker? Kat held her breath. No, she must have blinked, because when she looked again, there was the even beacon sweeping the shore. Kat went limp with relief and watched the rotating ray.

The light flickered again! No, she *wasn't* imagining it! A hissing, stuttering sound came from the top of the tower. What was happening? Kat's skin prickled. Something was terribly wrong! But the light had *never* failed. Another flicker. She froze in panic.

Suddenly the light went out! No! Everything was plunged into darkness. "Papa!" she cried out. "Papa!" She was on her own. All alone. No beacon. And a boat was out there in the night, floundering on the waves.

four

at's heart pounded. There was no time to get help. The boat was too close! It would never be able to navigate around the rocks in the dark. She pulled the foghorn. Its bleats were a deafening warning, but it couldn't guide the boat in.

What did Papa say to do if this happened? It had *never* happened. Her mind was racing, splintering. She couldn't think. She took a deep, shuddering breath. All right. Steady now. *Think!* The alarm bell!

Kat grabbed the kerosene lantern, its light wavering wildly in her shaking hand. She climbed up the second ladder. Her legs were trembling so, she almost stumbled. She *had* to stop shaking, the kerosene was sloshing around . . . Her hand on the bell's rope was all thumbs. She was clumsy with fear. She pulled the rope, up and down, with all her strength. The peals rang out.

Please, let it wake Papa! Could he hear it over the

roar of the storm? Even if he did, it would be too late! She had to do something *now*!

Kat held the lantern up against the glass facing the ocean. But at sea they'd see only a tiny light high up in the tower. Not enough to illuminate the rocks. Not enough to keep a boat from shattering on them. She had to do something else. But what? *What?*

Take the lantern to the beach, Kat thought. Show them where to come ashore. Their only chance. Hurry!

She grabbed the lantern, scrambled down both ladders, and ran out of the lighthouse. The rain drenched her immediately. She ran onto the strip of beach, tripping on fallen branches, fighting for her balance.

Kat held the lantern as high as her arm could reach. She ran from one end of the beach to the other. A moving light, to show them safe boundaries. Would they understand her signal? Oh please, God, let me guide them in! Please, not a shipwreck on the rocks!

Gasping for breath, she ran back and forth as best she could. Her feet were being sucked into the wet sand. Her blouse and her skirt were soaked and heavy. She remembered her slicker, still on the chair where she'd tossed it. She shivered and held the lantern up. Up and up. Her arm ached. It began to shake, every muscle trembling from effort. The wind threatened to knock her down. The lantern, that was the important thing, she had to hold it high. She couldn't stop, no matter what.

Lightning flashed through the sky. The boat was close enough to see. It was coming her way. Coming to the beach. Please, God, help me save them.

Time had become meaningless. Were minutes going by or hours? The storm, the boat, the rain. Her legs wouldn't run anymore. Walking. The lantern high. Lashing wind. Kat pushed wet hair from her eyes. Pain sliced from her shoulder to her wrist. She gritted her teeth. Walking. Can't trip. Hold the lantern up. Was it rain streaking down her cheeks or tears?

Through misty eyes, as though she was dreaming, Kat saw the boat wash ashore on the sand.

A man and a woman waded through swirling waist-high water and floundered onto the beach. And then she heard a voice behind her. Papa's voice. "Kat!"

"Papa!" Kat sagged against him. "Papa, the light went out!"

"I know, I heard the bell."

The man from the boat stared at her in amazement. "Was that you? Only you and that lantern? I can't believe a young girl—"

"I didn't think we'd make it," the woman sobbed. "Thank you. It was horrifying! Waves swamped the deck and . . . the thunder, the lightning . . ."

"Hush, Evelyn." The man put his arm around her. "We're all right now."

"Those terrible waves." Sheets of rain plastered the woman's hair to her head. Her eyes were wide with shock. "When everything went dark I was sure we were lost. I was sure it was the end."

"Kat, take these people to the cottage." Papa looked up at the lighthouse. "I need to see what happened." The wind snapped his oilcloth. "Please, go with my daughter. My wife has dry clothes and—"

"It was calm when we started. . . ." The man had to raise his voice to be heard over the pounding surf. "We're so grateful—"

"No time for talk now. I've got a light that needs fixing and you need to get out of this storm," Papa said. "Go on, Kat, hurry inside."

❧

In her attic bedroom, Kat dripped puddles on the wood-plank floor. She shivered. I'm safe now, she reminded herself. And those people are safe. And Ma will give us something hot to drink and . . . it's over. It's all over.

44

She peeled off her wet clothes. Her skirt and blouse were a soaked mess. And her shoes! What she wouldn't give for a hot bath now! But she didn't have the strength left to boil up the water and carry it to the washtub. Anyway, she wanted to see the couple. Evelyn and Kenneth Carstairs, Kat remembered. They had introduced themselves on the way to the cottage. Kat pulled on a heavy sweater and skirt. She toweled her hair. She couldn't stop shivering as she rushed downstairs.

The Carstairses were sitting at the table in front of steaming cups of tea. Papa's fisherman-knit sweater was miles too big for Mr. Carstairs. Mrs. Carstairs was wearing Ma's best cable cardigan. A blanket was draped over her shoulders.

"Katherine," Mrs. Carstairs said, "you were our guardian angel!"

Kat smiled and gulped down her tea. It burned her tongue, but the hot liquid took the chill from her body.

On the table, hurricane lamps flickered. A log was blazing in the fireplace. The Carstairses' cold-weather sailing gear lay in a pile on the hearth.

"We just closed our summer house in Shorehaven," Mrs. Carstairs said. "It was calm when we started out."

"The squall wasn't supposed to hit until morning,"

Mr. Carstairs said. "I thought it was still rounding Hatteras—"

"And we were heading home," Mrs. Carstairs continued. "If it wasn't for Katherine's bravery . . . I'm so sorry for all the trouble we've caused."

"No trouble at all," Ma said. "We'll put Mr. and Mrs. Carstairs in your room tonight." She touched Kat's shoulder. "Set up a bedroll for yourself in the boys' room. I think you need to go to bed."

Soon, Kat thought. She *was* getting sleepy. . . .

"I know it's late in the season, but Shorehaven is so lovely this time of year," Mrs. Carstairs was saying.

"We left in daylight, but we had trouble with a sail. One piece of bad luck after another, and it was twilight long before we could reach our destination," Mr. Carstairs said.

"We decided to dock at Cape Light for the night," Mrs. Carstairs added.

"Please don't think we're completely foolhardy," Mr. Carstairs said. "We're experienced sailors. We've been in any number of regattas along the New England coast and of course, the big one out of Newport." He sighed. "I was so sure we could beat the storm home to Boston."

Boston! Kat sat up straight, suddenly wide awake.

"You live in *Boston*? There's a famous art museum, isn't there?" As soon as she asked one question, ten more popped into Kat's head. "Do the Public Gardens really have swan boats? Do you ride trolleys? Is the Charles River—" Kat bit her lip. Ma's sharp look reminded her that asking too many questions wasn't polite.

Mrs. Carstairs smiled. "I don't know which to answer first."

"Kat, not now. I think everyone's exhausted." Ma glanced at the Carstairses. "We're all about ready to turn in."

Mr. Carstairs nodded. "It's been an eventful night."

But, Kat thought, it's my one chance to hear all about Boston! "Please, may I just ask—is Commonwealth Avenue—"

"Kat, go on to bed," Ma ordered.

"But, Ma—"

"Mr. and Mrs. Carstairs will be here in the morning," Ma added more softly. She handed Kat a hurricane lamp.

"And I'll be happy to tell you anything you want to know." Mrs. Carstairs smiled. "Good night, Katherine. You were wonderful. Thank you again."

"Sleep tight, Kat." Ma smiled.

Kat reluctantly went up to her room. She put on her

flannel nightgown and her fuzzy robe. Sunshine will keep me warm, she thought. Wait. Where was he? Why wasn't he curled up in his usual spot at the foot of her bed? Then she spotted the tip of a white tail poking out from under the bed.

"Come on out, scaredy dog. A big dog like you. . . . There's no lightning indoors, silly."

Sunshine wriggled out from under the bed. Kat could swear he looked embarrassed.

She took the bedroll and an extra quilt from the cupboard, the star quilt made by Grandma Williams long ago. She tiptoed into her brothers' room with Sunshine following close behind.

The light of her candle showed Todd asleep on the top bunk. He turned over, but he didn't wake up. James was in the lower bunk, his arms and legs spread out. His breath whistled softly. They'd slept through all the excitement!

Kat arranged her bedroll on the rag rug. Though she was worn out, she didn't lie down. Not yet. She wrapped the quilt around her and went to the window. She opened the shutters just a bit. All she could see was blackness.

She waited at the window; waited and worried. Then her heart jumped. The light went on! Its steady ray was revolving again.

Now she could rest.

She blew out the candle and burrowed into the comfort of the bedroll, but her thoughts drifted in all directions. The Carstairses. Boston. The lightning and her terror . . .

The door creaked open.

"Kat? Are you still awake?" Papa whispered.

"Yes."

He came close and squatted next to her. "Some wiring came loose," he whispered. "I soldered it. The light's working fine again."

"I know. I saw."

"I found your slicker on the chair. You could have used it."

"There wasn't time," she said.

"I know. . . . Kat, you saved those people. All by yourself." His callused hand stroked her cheek. "I'm proud of you, Kat. I couldn't be more proud."

Kat knew he was smiling at her in the dark. She smiled back and closed her eyes.

"I thank God you're safe, kitten. When I think of— "

Exhaustion washed over her and she didn't hear anything else.

The next thing Kat knew, the shutters were wide open and sunlight was streaming into the room. It was morning already! Todd and James were gone and their beds were neatly made. It had to be late. The Carstairses might have left!

Kat jumped up and threw on her bathrobe. She brushed her teeth slapdash and splashed some water over her face. There was no time to bother with braiding her hair. She tied back the tangled mass in one big bunch and clattered down the stairs.

If she'd missed the Carstairses, she would die!

h, good! Mrs. Carstairs was still here, sitting at the table.

Ma, at the stove, raised her eyebrows. "Kat! Your hair. A dress would—"

"Why didn't anyone wake me?"

"You needed your sleep," Ma said. "After last night."

Mrs. Carstairs smiled. "Besides, we'd never leave without saying good-bye to you."

Kat suddenly felt awkward. Why hadn't she stopped to get dressed? She was a complete mess and in front of a lady from Boston.

Mrs. Carstairs looked very different this morning. She was relaxed and her hair was in a neat bun. "Katherine, come sit with me," she said. "Your mother made the most delicious flapjacks."

Ma put a plate in front of Kat. "Here, I kept them warm for you."

"Where is everybody?"

"At Alveira's boatyard," Ma said, "getting work done on the boat."

"Thanks to you, there's very little damage," Mrs. Carstairs said. "It looks like we can sail home today without a problem."

Kat poured maple syrup on her pancakes, but her fork remained in midair. She was too excited to eat. "Home to Boston! Do you live right in the city?"

"Yes, we live in a row house close to Beacon Hill. It's an historic area. Well, Boston is an historic city. You can follow the path of Paul Revere's ride."

"And there's a famous art museum?"

Mrs. Carstairs smiled. "Yes, it has quite a collection—Corots, Turners, many of the Dutch masters, including van Eycks and some Rembrandts, I believe. Even some of those modern French painters . . . Impressionists, I think they're called. Renoir, Matisse . . ."

"Oh!" Kat said breathlessly. Oh, to see those paintings in person!

"Kat likes to draw," Ma said. "They always hang up her pictures in school." She gestured to the seascape over the fireplace. "That's one of Kat's."

"Why, that's lovely," Mrs. Carstairs said. She got up

for a closer look. "The way the sea blends into the sky, the shadows of the rocks . . . You are remarkably talented."

"Oh! Oh, thank you!" This was a lady from Boston who would *know*! Well, maybe she was just being polite. But she didn't have to say "remarkably"—so maybe she meant it! Kat was filled with a warm glow.

"Are there . . . are there any famous women artists in Boston?"

"Women artists?" Mrs. Carstairs frowned. "Let me see . . . I can't think of any. I suppose women in art are mostly the artists' models or wives," Mrs. Carstairs said.

"Oh." Kat felt heavy with disappointment. "Maybe . . . maybe it'll be different by the time I grow up."

"I hope so." Mrs. Carstairs looked closely at Kat. "Do you want to be a *professional* artist?"

Katherine nodded, embarrassed. Did Mrs. Carstairs think that was silly? Or even worse, hopeless?

"Perhaps women will be taken more seriously if we ever get the vote," Mrs. Carstairs said. "It's beginning. . . . I've seen suffragettes parading on Commonwealth Avenue. Of course, a lot of people make fun of them. Some even throw rotten fruit!"

"They're so brave," Kat said. "I'd like to be a suffragette."

"Kat, you don't mean that!" Ma said.

"Commonwealth Avenue is the main street, isn't it?" Kat asked.

"Yes," said Mrs. Carstairs. "But it's getting too crowded and busy, with more and more of those automobiles. Too noisy, and they really do scare the horses."

Ma put an arm around Kat. "I hope my daughter isn't pestering you with too many questions."

"Oh, no, not at all. It's nice to meet someone so bright and curious," Mrs. Carstairs said.

"I'd give *anything* to live in Boston! There'd be so much to see!"

"I hope you'll come to visit. I'd love to show you around," Mrs. Carstairs said. Suddenly she exclaimed, "Mary Cassatt!"

"Pardon?" Kat asked.

"I just remembered. Mary Cassatt is a famous woman artist. She was discovered by Degas. She's an American but she's lived in France for many years."

So there *is* someone, Kat thought. Wait till I tell Lizabeth and Amanda!

Kat's flapjacks were cold and forgotten. And later— when Papa and Mr. Carstairs came in, when the boys made their noisy entrance, when the Carstairses were getting ready to leave, when the good-byes and thank-you's were said—Mrs. Carstairs's words were still going round and round in Kat's head. Visions of Boston danced before her eyes.

Somehow I'll get there, she thought, no matter what it takes.

<h1 style="text-align:center">~*six*~</h1>

 fter the Carstairses left, Kat helped Ma hang the laundry on the line outside the cottage.

"A nice sunny day," Ma said through the clothespin between her teeth as she lifted a sheet from the laundry basket.

Kat took the other end of the sheet and fastened it to the line. Once the clothespin held it securely, Kat took a step back. She hated it when a breeze flapped wet laundry into her face!

"Look at the ocean, Ma. You'd never know we had a storm." The sea was calm. Waves splashed lazily against rocks that didn't look menacing today. Off in the distance, boats were out again. Except for some broken tree branches on the ground, there were few reminders of last night's nightmare.

"Your father said some of the roof shingles were broken." Ma shook out one of Todd's shirts.

Kat pinned a pillowcase to the line and glanced back at the cottage. She couldn't see much of the roof from where she stood.

"He'll take a closer look when he gets back," Ma said. Papa had taken the horse and wagon to see if there had been damage in town. "I hope everyone came through without trouble."

Kat and Ma automatically took opposite ends of the larger items. Sheets, towels, clothespins, shirts, napkins, clothespins. Kat didn't mind hanging the wash; it was the ironing she hated. When the laundry was not quite dry, it would be time to heat the five irons at the fireplace. As soon as one iron cooled too much to be of any use, Ma needed the next hot iron. It was Kat's job to keep them coming. Ma was teaching her to iron. It was maddening. If Kat was careful not to scorch their things, she couldn't iron them smooth enough. And shirts were impossible! What was the point, anyway, if everything was going to get wrinkled all over again? Though Kat had to admit she loved sleeping on freshly ironed sheets smelling of sunshine and sea breeze.

Women's work was no fun. Kat knew exactly the kind of work she wanted to do. Mary Cassatt, she thought. She just had to see her paintings! If there was one famous woman artist, there could be others. And one of them could be *Katherine Williams*!

"Kat! You're letting that towel trail on the ground!"

"Oh! Sorry." Kat quickly pinned it to the line. Tablecloths, shirts, clothespins . . . "Ma, Mrs. Carstairs was so nice, wasn't she?"

"Yes, I liked her very much. Kat, for you to come downstairs in a bathrobe—it just wasn't proper."

"I was so anxious not to miss the Carstairses. . . . I'm sorry, I didn't stop to think."

Kat held up two corners of a cotton blanket and Ma held the other two. They moved together to hang it.

"Kat, you're growing up and certain things are expected of a young lady. You *have* to stop to think. You have to be less impulsive and—"

"I know, Ma. I'll try. I really will."

"Last night, you showed so much character and responsibility. A grown man couldn't have handled it better. I'm very proud of you. But sometimes I don't know what you're going to do next." Ma picked up the empty laundry basket and balanced it against her hip. "And there was something Aunt Sue mentioned to me. Something about finding you buried in leaves? What was that about?"

Kat shrugged. "Um . . . nothing."

Ma raised her eyebrows.

"Nothing important," Kat mumbled. She whirled around at the sound of approaching wheels. "Here comes Papa!" She ran to the horse and wagon on the lane and Ma followed.

"Hello, Papa!" Kat petted the horse's velvety nose.

"What happened in town?" Ma asked.

"Bad news. The Hallorans' barn was hit by lightning." Papa jumped off the wagon. "Burned to the ground."

"Oh, that's terrible." Ma shook her head. "I'll call on Mrs. Halloran after church tomorrow."

"Bad as it was, thank goodness it didn't spread to their house," Papa said. "And we lost that big maple by the side of the courthouse. It's covering the village green."

"That was a beautiful old tree," Ma said.

"It'll be a job to cut it up and haul it away. I was just coming back for my ax." Papa sighed. "It's a shame. Well, there'll be more firewood for everybody this winter."

"What about the Hallorans' cows?" Kat asked.

"They made it out. They're stabled at the Whites' for now." Papa was heading for the cottage. "So there'll be a barn raising next week."

"And a barn dance after?" Kat asked.

"Next Saturday night."

"That will be such fun!"

Kat loved square dancing, loved whirling in circles with the caller's "Swing your lady, swing her down, allemande left, promenade to town. . . ." She wished she didn't have to wait a whole week for it. But it would take the week for Mr. Halloran and his boys to assemble the timbers and have them ready to go. Then on Saturday, all the men would come to raise the framework into place, something that one family could never do alone. All the women would bring pots and pans of their best recipes in the evening. Ma would bring her special potato salad for sure, and probably apple pie. . . .

"I ran into Amanda and Lizabeth in town," Papa said.

"I can't wait to see them," Kat said. "I have so much to tell them!"

"You can tell them after church tomorrow," Ma said. "Kat, please see about collecting the eggs."

In church on Sunday, Kat turned every once in a while to see if that boy was still staring at Amanda. But she paid attention to Reverend Morgan's sermon, too. His words always inspired her to be the very best person she could.

After the service, Kat saw Amanda holding Hannah's hand, and Lizabeth waiting for her at the bottom of the church steps. She was dying to run right to them, but she was expected to file out with her family. Reverend Morgan stood at the door to say a few words to everyone as they left.

Kat didn't know how he did it—he remembered the name of every single child in the congregation. Even all ten of the Hallorans, and Kat wasn't sure the Hallorans themselves could keep them straight! Reverend Morgan was such a kind man, Kat thought. He was always calling on people who were sick or troubled, and helping in every possible way. The only fault Kat could see was that he didn't have much time left over for Amanda and Hannah.

After he greeted Ma and Papa, the Reverend's dark, serious eyes were on Kat. "You're the talk of the town, Katherine."

"I am?" Kat was startled. What did I do *now*?

"Saving a life earns a special place in heaven."

Oh, the Carstairses! Kat blushed with pleasure. "Thank you, Reverend Morgan."

He smiled at her. "I see Amanda and Lizabeth are waiting very impatiently. . . .Well, Todd, how is that project coming along?"

61

Kat flew down the steps to her friends.

"We couldn't wait to see you!" Lizabeth said.

"Out in the lightning!" Amanda said. "Weren't you scared?"

"I wasn't scared," Kat said. She looked at her friends. "I was *terrified*."

"You're a hero." Hannah's little face was awestruck.

"And wait till I tell you—Mr. and Mrs. Carstairs are from *Boston*," Kat continued. In a rush of words, she tried to make them see all that Mrs. Carstairs had described. "And there *is* a famous woman artist. Mrs. Carstairs told me. Mary Cassatt!"

"I've never heard of her," Lizabeth said.

"That doesn't mean she's not famous," Amanda said.

"Anyway, I have some news, too." Lizabeth paused dramatically until the other girls stared at her, waiting. "I know who bought the house across the way from Amanda's."

"Go on!" Amanda said. "Who are they?"

"They're from New York City. Dr. and Mrs. Forbes."

"Why would they ever come here all the way from New York City?" Kat asked. New York was even bigger than Boston. It had to be full of wonders.

"Mrs. Forbes's sister lives in Cape Light. Maybe that's why. You know the Claytons, don't you? They own those stables out past the orchard? Well, Mrs. Clayton is Mrs. Forbes's sister." Lizabeth was puffed up with importance for knowing all the facts. "Anyway, they're going to turn part of the Reynolds house into Dr. Forbes's medical office and waiting room. They're moving in March."

"Cape Light needs a doctor," Amanda said. "Maybe if my mother had . . ." She glanced at Hannah and bit her lip.

Kat knew what Amanda was thinking. But Annie Albright was an excellent midwife, everyone said so, and later the doctor from Cranberry came. . . .

"And the Forbeses have a daughter," Lizabeth continued.

"Is she six years old?" Hannah asked hopefully.

"No. One daughter, that's all. Her name is Rose. And guess what? She's around our age. Fourteen."

"I hope she's nice," Amanda said.

"I hope she's fashionable," Lizabeth said.

Typical Lizabeth, Kat thought.

"Rose is a pretty name," Kat said. Maybe one day she would have a friend from a big city. She couldn't wait until March to meet her.

seven

iss Cotter, the teacher, said, "If you've finished your work, you must wait silently with your hands folded on your lap until I come around to you." Kat couldn't really blame Miss Cotter; with sixty students in grades one through nine in the same room, she had to keep the class in control. Especially with the assistant teacher, Miss Harding, out for the week with influenza.

But how could Kat *possibly* remain quiet for hours? She always had so much to say!

The littlest children—Hannah, Mary Margaret, Betsy, and Joseph—whispered while they were working with wooden alphabet blocks. Todd was always good, but James got into trouble for talking to Roger and Francis.

That week everyone was thinking about the barn dance. The boys talked about the food. "I hope Mrs.

White brings that lemon meringue pie." "I love ice cream. You think someone will bring ice cream?" "Dummy, it would melt."

"James and Francis!" Miss Cotter said. "Maybe your penmanship would be neater if you talked less and *concentrated more.*"

Well, Kat thought, at least Miss Cotter didn't rap their knuckles with her ruler—that hurt!

Kat, Lizabeth, and Amanda sat at a table with Joanna, Mabel, and Grace. They were practicing their sewing: two small running stitches forward and one stitch back to make a tight seam. Amanda's seam was neat and even. Kat didn't have the patience. Her running stitches galloped ahead.

"Much too large, Katherine," Miss Cotter corrected. "Please take them out and start again."

"Why do we have to learn this, Miss Cotter?" Lizabeth put down her practice cloth. "You can make a tighter seam with a sewing machine. With your foot on the treadle, it goes so fast."

"Not everyone has a sewing machine, Lizabeth," Miss Cotter said.

While Miss Cotter was busy teaching division to the third graders, Lizabeth whispered, "What's everyone wearing?"

"To the barn dance? I got the prettiest dress from Montgomery Ward. It just came last week," Amanda said. "It's dark red—the catalog calls it burgundy—and it has puffy shoulders and long, tight sleeves and a big sash."

"I don't understand clothes from a catalog." Lizabeth sniffed. "They're made in factories, with one person just doing sleeves and another just doing collars and . . . I don't see how they can possibly fit. I always have at least two fittings."

"Mine fits," Amanda said.

"I'm wearing my Alice-blue dress," Lizabeth said.

The whole country was in love with the president's beautiful oldest daughter, Alice; she was so lively and full of fun. Kat had read in the newspaper that Teddy Roosevelt himself had said, "I can do one of two things. I can be President of the United States or I can control Alice. I cannot possibly do both." That had to be said with a smile, of course. Alice was the ideal American girl.

"It has a wonderfully wide skirt," Lizabeth continued, "so when I swing around, it'll twirl and twirl. It has the tiniest tucks in the front. And I'm getting a rat for my hair."

"A rat?" Grace laughed. "Watch it doesn't bite you!"

"You know what I mean," Lizabeth said impatiently. "That padding to puff up my hair on top for a pompadour."

"Momma says pompadours are for older girls," Joanna said.

"I don't care—I'm having one for the dance," Lizabeth said.

Lizabeth was in a hurry to grow up, Kat thought. Next thing, she'd be lacing herself up in corsets! How could Ma and Aunt Sue move—or even breathe—in them?

"What are you wearing, Kat?" Lizabeth asked.

Kat shrugged. She didn't care much about fashion. Lizabeth would get all excited about her new dresses, made by a dressmaker with special fabric from the city. Amanda ordered hers from Sears and Montgomery Ward. She loved looking through the catalogs. Ma made Kat's dresses from Butterick patterns. She always picked the most durable fabrics from the bolts at the general store.

"My Sunday dress, I guess." Kat hadn't given it much thought before. But was it too plain? "You know the striped one with the pinafore? Do you think—"

"Lizabeth and Katherine!" Miss Cotter called. "I see your mouths moving but not your needles."

❧

At recess on Wednesday, Amanda was helping Hannah and her friends skip rope.

Kat roamed the schoolyard with Lizabeth and Grace. She spotted James with the big boys who were playing mumblety-peg.

"James!" she called. He knew he wasn't allowed to play that game! He was too young to be flipping a pocket knife. There was a chance he'd flip it right into his foot instead of the ground!

James made a pleading face at her, but Kat shook her head "no." She kept her eye on him until he wandered over to see Roger's new wooden top.

". . . and gray suede boots with tiny little buttons going past my ankle and . . ." Grace was saying.

They were *still* talking about clothes. What a waste of recess! Soon it would be too cold to play outdoors.

"See you later." Kat headed for a group playing tag.

Lizabeth followed her. "Wait, Kat. I was thinking . . . I have a new dress. It's sort of jade green and it's really pretty, with the nicest ruffle at the bottom," Lizabeth said. "But the color's all wrong for me. It makes me look pale as a ghost."

What was Lizabeth talking about? She looked perfectly fine in green.

"It's a perfect color for *you*, though," Lizabeth continued. "Want to have it? You could wear it to the dance."

"Your dress?"

"I'll bring it to school for you tomorrow," Lizabeth said. "I can't wait to see how you look in it!"

"Thank you!" Kat gave her cousin a big hug. "Thank you, Lizabeth!" Kat didn't care much about clothes, not really. But when she heard Amanda and Lizabeth talking about their new dresses this morning . . . it would be nice to have a new dress to wear. And all of Lizabeth's things were so *pretty*!

⚘

Finally, it was Saturday night!

Lizabeth's dress was the most wonderful color, Kat thought, as if she'd mixed vermilion green with just a touch of cerulean blue. It had a deep ruffle at the bottom that swished around her feet. Kat couldn't help stroking the fabric—it was the smoothest, softest wool. It fit perfectly, too. It made her feel . . . well, different, in a new, good way.

Now that she was almost thirteen, it wouldn't hurt to do something more than braids, would it? That beautiful dress needed something more. Not a pompadour, but . . .

"Ma, would you curl my hair?"

Ma looked pleased. "You've never let me before. You really have beautiful hair, Kat. Come into the kitchen."

Ma heated the curling iron in the stove and wound strands of Kat's hair around it. Ugh, that thing was hot and it pulled and took forever.

"No more!" Kat said.

"I can't stop now," Ma said. "You can't have one side curled and the other straight."

"All right," Kat grumbled. "Are we almost finished?"

"Almost." Ma smiled. "They say you have to suffer for beauty."

"Almost" took a long time—but when Ma was done, Kat's hair flowed down her back in long, soft ringlets. As she entered the barn with Ma, Todd, and James, she found herself walking more slowly, letting the ruffle flutter gently around her legs. She felt pretty!

She heard the toe-tapping music and the fiddler calling, "Swing in the center, then break that pair; lady goes on, and gent stays there. . . ."

Papa met them at the door. He took Ma's hand and whirled her into the square dance. He was a surprisingly graceful dancer, even with his limp. Todd and James rushed to join the crowd at the long table on the side. It was piled high from end to end: potato salad, cole slaw, fried fish, fried chicken, beef hash, green beans, baked beans, a whole ham, deep-dish apple pie (that was Ma's), peach cobbler, and on and on. James was helping himself to a huge chunk of Mrs. White's famous lemon meringue pie. Out of Ma's sight, he always went straight for dessert.

Kat made her way through the barn, skirting around the lively dancers. The reverend was swinging a thrilled, laughing Hannah off her feet. Neighbors mingled on the sidelines and little children spun each other around with abandon. She said hello to many freshly scrubbed class-mates and quickly found Amanda and Lizabeth.

"I don't think he'll be here," Amanda was saying.

"Well, he is," Lizabeth said. "Right there!"

Kat followed her glance. There was that boy from church standing across the room. He was tall, with brown hair and a firm chin. Amanda was right—he *was* handsome!

"Don't look," Amanda pleaded.

"He's staring at you," Kat said.

"Is he? Don't look, Kat!"

"And . . . he's coming over!" Kat said. She heard Amanda catch her breath.

And then he stood in front of them. He shifted awk-wardly from foot to foot. Amanda looked at him, looked down, looked at him, looked away. If they're *both* going to be that shy, Kat thought, we'll be standing here in total silence forever!

"Hello, I'm Kat," she said.

"And I'm Lizabeth."

"I'm Amanda." Her words came out breathlessly.

"I know," he said. "Amanda Morgan. I—uh—found out."

Amanda blushed.

There was a long pause.

"You must have a name, too," Kat finally said to the boy.

"I . . . um . . ."

Had he forgotten his own name, Kat wondered. She and Lizabeth could have been invisible. His eyes were glued to Amanda.

"Um . . . do you think . . . um . . . Would you like to dance?" he asked.

Amanda nodded. She seemed to have lost the ability to speak, too. Kat grinned as she watched him take Amanda's hand and lead her to the dance area.

"Well, he's handsome," Lizabeth said. "I'll say that much for him."

"They look nice together," Kat said. "But does love

have to make you senseless?" Both girls giggled.

Kat would have kept watching them, but Billy from school asked her to dance. Then Mark, the blacksmith's son, who'd been her friend forever. Promenade. Do-si-do. Kat danced and danced, with Papa and then with Todd. With Mr. Thomas from the general store and more friends from school. To "Turkey in the Straw." To "The Arkansas Traveler." "Allemande left and allemande right," the fiddler called. Kat whirled and twirled, hair flying behind her, loving every minute of it. Finally, flushed and perspiring, she collapsed on a chair at the side.

That's when she saw Amanda. She was still dancing with that boy, in the center of the Virginia reel line. Her smile was radiant. Everything about Amanda was shining.

Kat wished she had someone to like, too. Someone she hadn't known her whole life, someone who could make her glow like that.

Lizabeth collapsed on the chair next to Kat's. Strands of hair were escaping from her pompadour. "I had the best time, didn't you?"

"Uh-huh." Kat glanced around the barn. It was emptying out. Soon Papa would be taking them home. Some of the women were gathering their pots and dishes. Her gaze stopped at a boy standing next to her cousin Christopher. She'd never seen him before. His eyes were a startling blue.

"Who's that?" Kat asked. "With your brother?" He had the blackest, shiniest hair.

"Oh, that's Michael," Lizabeth said. "Chris's friend from Cranberry. He's staying over this weekend."

Kat wished she had seen him earlier. She wished he had asked her to dance.

The next day the girls gathered in the tower. Half of the fun of the dance was talking about it later!

Amanda sat on the rag rug with her smoke-gray Sunday skirt billowing out all around her. ". . . and his name is Jed Langford," she was saying. "Isn't that the most beautiful name you ever heard?"

"It's a *name*, Amanda." Lizabeth had picked the chair nearest the warm stove. Kat was stoking the coals. It was cold even in the daytime now.

"He has four older brothers," Amanda went on, "and he *is* a deckhand, but he plans to be the captain of his own ship someday." Her eyes were glowing green. "And he has a pet goat and—"

"He seemed awfully shy last night," Lizabeth said.

"Oh, no, not at all—not once we got to talking," Amanda said.

"Looks like someone is going to come courting," Kat teased.

"Father would never allow that." Amanda's face fell. "I'm too young for courting. Not until I'm at least fifteen."

They had dozens of other things to talk about, but there was one sentence that Kat replayed in her mind later, over and over again.

"Michael asked Chris about you last night," Lizabeth had told her.

"He did?" Kat shrugged. She tried to sound just mildly curious. "What did he say?"

"'Who was that pretty redhead with your sister?'"

"He said that?"

"His exact words."

Who was that pretty redhead! Kat hugged the words to herself. That was *me*! Cranberry was close by. Maybe, cross her fingers, maybe she would see Michael again.

~eight~

by early November, it was freezing. Kat rushed home from school. She kept her hands in her coat pockets, but her fingertips still felt frozen. Mitten weather, she thought. She'd have to remember to wear them to school tomorrow.

She ran into the cottage, thinking of the blazing logs that would be in the fireplace. The door banged shut behind her.

"Kat," Ma said, "please don't slam the door."

"Oops, sorry." She didn't want to think about how often she'd been reminded to close the door quietly.

"You left your scarf and mittens home again."

"I know. I forgot." Kat shrugged off her coat.

"Where are the boys?"

"Coming along the lane. They've been dawdling all the way."

"I received a lovely gift from the Carstairses." Ma

opened a white cardboard box. "Look at this tablecloth, Kat. Isn't it lovely? Please don't touch unless your hands are absolutely clean. They shouldn't have; it wasn't at all necessary."

"It's really beautiful," Kat said. The fine beige linen had delicate lace inserts.

"And they sent something for you, too. On your bed."

"For me?" Kat ran up the stairs two at a time. The box on her bed was covered by the most beautiful paper, gold with red and blue designs. She'd never seen such fancy gift paper. In Cape Light, people wrapped presents in white paper from the general store or the bookshop.

Kat couldn't wait to open the package—but she did it slowly so she wouldn't tear that special paper, Then she folded it carefully to save it. A box of chocolates! Before dinner? Oh, well. She couldn't resist.

She popped a chocolate into her mouth. Mmmm, it had a delicious creamy filling that tasted of vanilla. Then another. This one had a different filling, cherry. She wanted to try them all, though she knew she really should save some for her family. Maybe just one more, just to see . . . That's when she noticed the envelope. A letter from the Carstairses!

Dear Katherine,

There is really no way to thank you for saving our lives. We owe everything to your quick thinking and courage.

We were most impressed by how very bright, talented, and curious you are. A close friend of ours is the headmaster of the Bartholomew School in Boston and we told him all about you. The Bartholomew School is well known for excellence and has an extremely selective admittance process. However, the headmaster agreed to admit you for the January semester if you would like to go. The school has challenging academics and an outstanding art program—we thought that might be of special interest to you.

They would waive room and board; that leaves the tuition of $50 per semester. Your tuition and the enclosed application, to be sent directly to the school, would be due by December 15th to hold a place for you for January. Of course, you'll want to talk this over with your parents and we'd be happy to answer any questions.

If you would rather remain in your school in Cape Light, we still hope that you'll visit us in Boston. We'd be delighted to welcome you to our city and our home.

With sincerest thanks,
Evelyn and Kenneth Carstairs

Katherine sat on her bed, stunned. She read the

Carstairses' words again. For a moment, she couldn't breathe.

Then she jumped up. "Ma! Papa! Everybody!" she screamed.

She heard Papa running toward the stairs. "Kat? What's wrong?"

"Nothing's wrong!" She raced down. Sunshine ran toward her, barking. "Everything's right! Everything's wonderful!"

Papa, Ma, Todd, and James had gathered at the foot of the stairs. "What?" "What is it?" "Kat, say something!"

"Papa, read this!" Kat's hand was shaking as she handed him the letter.

Papa read it. He frowned and silently passed it to Ma.

"What happened?" Todd said. "Isn't anyone going to tell me?" He grabbed the letter from Ma when she finished.

"That's a very nice gesture," Papa said. "But—"

"You're so young; you belong here with your family," Ma said. "Kat, write them a note. Say you appreciate the thought—"

"Appreciate the thought?" Kat exploded. "I'm going to Boston!"

"Kat, you know that's impossible," Papa's voice had become very quiet.

"It's not impossible! It's my dream come true!" Kat looked at their faces. "Why isn't everyone happy?"

"I'm happy," James piped up.

"I just wish they'd written to us first," Ma said, "instead of getting you all excited."

"Of course I'm excited! Why shouldn't I be?" Kat trailed Papa and Ma to the kitchen table. "They said they'll answer any questions you have. . . ."

James wandered away. Todd stayed in the doorway, listening.

"Fifty dollars for tuition. And that's just for one semester." Papa sighed as he sank into his chair. "Kat, we don't have that kind of money."

"Even if we were willing to send you so far away," Ma added.

"But Papa, they'll waive my room and board!" Kat sat down opposite him. "You read the letter. There's an outstanding art program! I'll get art training—the training I need and—and I'll live in a big city and I'll . . . it's everything I've always wanted!"

"What about the lighthouse?" Ma said. "We do need you here."

"I could take Kat's shift," Todd said. "If she went to Boston."

Kat looked at Todd gratefully. She knew he'd much rather read or play in his room. He was on her side.

"No, Kat. I can't pay for a private school," Papa said.

"It's my big opportunity!" Kat said. "You *can't* take it away from me! You can't!"

"Do you think I want to take anything away from you? Don't you know I'd give you the moon if I could?"

Kat had never seen her father look so defeated. It broke her heart to see it. She knew she should stop now—but she couldn't.

"All I'm asking for is a good school and—and a chance to make something of myself! Fifty dollars. That's not the moon!"

"I didn't raise you to be disrespectful. Stop badgering your father right now." Ma had placed a protective hand on Papa's shoulder. "You can make something of yourself without the Bartholomew School."

"But I *have* to go!"

"We get the cottage for free because we're the lighthouse keepers." Papa sounded very tired. "But we're responsible for maintaining it—you know that. And some months our stipend barely stretches to cover our expenses."

"But they'll waive room and board—"

"I'm sorry. The answer is no. End of discussion."

Kat didn't want to make her father feel bad but she couldn't give up. "We can save fifty dollars somehow, there must be a way and—"

"That's enough, Kat! Leave your father alone," Ma said.

"And I'll eat clam chowder every night of the week, I don't care, I don't need clothes or—"

"Katherine, I've always provided for this family!" Papa's voice had turned icy. He never called her "Katherine" unless he was furious. "There's always food on the table and shoes for my children. You've never wanted for anything!"

"I didn't mean . . ." Kat whispered. "I just thought . . . there must be a way we can—"

"Enough!" Papa thundered.

Two red circles formed on Kat's cheeks. She had hurt Papa's pride and she felt guilty. But he was hurting her, too. He wouldn't even listen!

She bit her lip as she helped Ma snap the beans.

Later, the dinner conversation flowed around and past her, and she didn't say a word. Papa said there might be more damage than broken shingles. Ma hoped not. Papa had to check the roof more carefully. Todd wanted to enter the spelling bee this year. James said his *real* best friend was Francis. . . . Everyone was acting normal, as if her dreams hadn't just been crushed!

It would be too terrible for this opportunity to come, just to be snatched away! She glanced at her father. All right, fifty dollars was more than he could afford. . . .

"Kat!"

"What, James?"

"I said, 'Please pass the bread.' *Twice.*"

Kat passed the basket. She nibbled at her food without tasting it. If only there was less tuition for Papa to pay. . . . If only . . . Maybe she could earn some of it herself!

Papa was starting on the bread pudding, his favorite dessert. He looked relaxed now. He was never angry for long. Did she dare?

"Papa?" Kat said.

He turned toward her.

"If it was less than fifty dollars—"

"But it's not," he interrupted. "Stop it, Kat. I want to eat my dinner in peace."

"Please, just listen," Kat pleaded. "What if I earn half of it by myself? If you only had to pay twenty-five dollars? Then could I go to the Bartholomew School?"

"How can you possibly earn twenty-five dollars? And by December fifteenth?" Papa said.

"But if I do," Kat said. "*If.*"

"If pigs had wings, they'd all fly." Papa poured fresh cream on his pudding.

"Kat, I think you need to give up on this," Ma said.

"Papa, if I have twenty-five dollars by December fifteenth, would you pay the rest?"

He sighed. "I suppose. But I don't see how you—"

Kat caught her breath. "Do you promise?"

"You certainly know how to wear a man down, Kat." Papa passed his hand across his forehead. "All right, I promise. If you can come up with twenty-five dollars, I guess I can, too."

Kat jumped up out of her seat and hugged him. "Thank you, Papa! Thank you!"

"I hope you're not planning to rob your uncle's bank." Joking, Kat knew, was her father's way of making up for yelling at her.

"No." Kat giggled.

She ran upstairs to write a letter to the Carstairses.

She wrote slowly, concentrating on good penmanship. She was very careful to avoid splotches when she dipped her pen in the ink bottle.

Dear Mr. and Mrs. Carstairs,

Thank you very much for the delicious chocolates. I love chocolate and these are the best I've ever had. And thank you for the wonderful opportunity to go to the Bartholomew School. I'm very happy to accept the offer and I'll send the application and the tuition to the school by December 15th.

Kat chewed on the pen as she thought about what to write next. She reread her last sentence and suddenly a prickly feeling came over her. How was she ever going to earn twenty-five dollars? It was already November seventh and she had no plan at all!

∼*nine*∼

The next morning, Kat walked to school with Todd. For a long stretch of Lighthouse Lane, they were quiet, deep in their own thoughts. James ran ahead with his friend Francis.

"I can give you five dollars," Todd suddenly said.

"What? What do you mean?"

"For that school. I have the five dollars I saved up from yard work last summer. And from my paper route."

"Oh, Todd! I can't take your money," Kat said. "You worked so hard for it."

"I want to give it to you," he said. "You'd help me out, wouldn't you? If I needed it? For something really important?"

"You know I would." Kat looked at him and smiled. "You really understand, don't you? I think you're the only one in the whole family who does. Todd . . . thank you."

Todd nodded. "You're welcome. Now you only need twenty."

"It sounds like a lot less that way, doesn't it? Thank you! I promise I'll pay you back someday."

"See, I have a dream, too, but I never say anything to anyone. All my friends want to be captains of their own boats or own their own farms. I want something different."

Her brother was the quiet, thoughtful one in the family. "What's your dream?" Kat often wondered what was going on in his mind. "Come on, Todd, what is it?"

"I want to be an inventor! Like Alexander Graham Bell and Thomas Watson. Well, they've already invented the telephone . . ." Todd grinned. "Beat me to it! But I want to be an inventor like them and I'd think up my *own* ideas."

They left Lighthouse Lane and turned south onto William McKinley Road. Kat checked on James. He was still in sight, running toward the school with his friend.

"See, everything's changing so fast now," Todd said. "Electricity, flying machines . . . Something new every single day! I bet there'll be things no one can even imagine yet. So I want to invent some of them. Well, what do you think? You think it sounds impossible or conceited or—?"

"It sounds just right. I think you can do just about

anything you put your mind to." Kat took Todd's hand and squeezed it. "Thank you for telling me about your dream."

৶৶৶

Lizabeth and Amanda were standing on the front steps of the school. Miss Cotter hadn't rung the big brass bell yet.

"Twenty dollars?" Amanda's eyes opened wide when Kat told them her news. "That's a lot!"

Kat's shoulders sagged. "I don't even know where to start."

"We'll help you," Amanda said.

"Here's how my father says you make money," Lizabeth said. "You make a product that everyone wants and sell it a fair price."

Miss Cotter was in the doorway, swinging the bell in her hand.

"I don't have a product." Kat slowly started up the steps.

"Girls, come along!" Miss Cotter called.

"Don't worry, we'll find a way," Amanda said.

Miss Cotter kept them busy all morning. She drilled them on the multiplication tables. Then the older boys did woodwork while the girls sewed. Miss Cotter asked

Kat to help the second graders draw with crayons. Crayons were new to Cape Light. Kat didn't like them that much. They were too waxy and didn't blend well. At least they didn't drip all over the second graders the way paint did.

Amanda, across the room at the sewing table, mouthed, "I have an idea."

"What?" Kat mouthed back.

There was no chance to talk. Everyone, except for the very youngest, was asked to line up in front of the room to practice for the spelling bee.

"Children, this year the spelling bee will be held in the courthouse! It's going to be a big event."

A buzz of excitement filled the room. Everyone in town would come out to be entertained by the spelling bee.

"The Cranberry schools will be taking part, too," Miss Cotter continued. "And Mrs. Cornell will be donating a prize from the Pelican Street Bookshop."

She'd probably be gone by then, Kat thought, but it didn't matter. There had to be a lot more going on in Boston than a spelling bee! She wasn't a great speller anyway.

Finally, it was recess. Kat and Lizabeth ran to Amanda in the schoolyard. "What's your idea? What is it?"

"*Everyone* loves ice cream," Amanda said. "It's the perfect product!"

"But how can we—?" Lizabeth started.

"There's a lady named Nancy Johnson—I read about her in the *Saturday Evening Post*," Amanda continued. "She invented a hand-cranked freezer that allows ice cream to be made at home—very easily, the article said."

"That's brilliant!" Kat said.

Lizabeth frowned. "But who has a hand-cranked freezer?"

"Cranking just means turning it, doesn't it?" Kat said. "Stir it, that's all it means."

Lizabeth brightened. "And freezing—ice from the icebox."

"All we need is cream, ice, and flavoring, and we'll keep mixing until it turns into ice cream," Amanda said. "Delicious!"

"And profitable," Lizabeth added. "Everyone loves ice cream."

"Exactly." Amanda smiled.

"If we sell it on the village green and charge fifteen cents, and suppose that thirty people come by . . . I bet we get lots of repeat customers," Kat said. "Thirty times fifteen is—"

"We can't charge that much," Amanda said. "At the restaurant in Cranberry, ice cream costs ten cents a dish."

"All right. Ten cents," Kat agreed.

"Thirty times ten . . . three dollars in one afternoon," Lizabeth said.

"It's November eighth—I have plenty of afternoons left before December fifteenth!" Kat felt as though a huge weight had been lifted from her shoulders.

"I bet you'll have a lot extra left over," Lizabeth said. "You could buy beautiful elbow-length kid gloves or . . ."

"We should get started right away," Kat said.

"My house tomorrow after school," Lizabeth said. "Mother is taking Christopher and Tracy to the dentist and it's the cook's day off, so the kitchen will be ours. I'll ask Ada to get lots of cream for us before she leaves."

"I'll arrange for Hannah to play at Mary Margaret's tomorrow," Amanda said.

"Wonderful!" Kat beamed. Anything was possible when good friends put their heads together.

❧

"First, the bowl." Lizabeth reached to the top of the cupboard for a large, deep bowl.

"Next, the cream," Kat said. There were three big

pitchers. Ada had actually followed Lizbeth's instructions and had all that cream ready and waiting for them. The girls poured it into the yellow ceramic bowl. "Well, that's easy!"

"Now for the ice," Amanda said.

They looked at the large blocks of ice in the icebox. "We've got to chip some off," Lizbeth said.

That wasn't so easy. They tried chipping it with kitchen knives but it was too rock-hard. Lizbeth found a hammer in a drawer and they took turns swinging it. Shards of ice flew wildly onto the floor. The girls slipped and slid.

"We *can't* use it off the floor," Amanda said.

"But there's so much of it, all our effort is wasted. . . ." Kat moaned.

"We *can't*."

"All right. I know what, put clean towels down to catch it." Kat banged the hammer and loosened some big chunks. They were collected and added to the bowl.

Lizbeth took some big swings at the ice and massaged her arm. "I think that's enough."

"No, we need more to make it freeze." Kat landed the hammer again and again. She switched from her right hand to her left. Pieces of ice of all sizes swam in the cream. "Now *that* looks like enough."

"What flavor do we want?" Lizabeth rummaged in the cupboard. "There's strawberry jam and apple jelly and . . . squash preserves, no! Wait, here's some baker's chocolate! The package says it's from San Francisco."

"Oh, good, everybody likes chocolate," Amanda said.

They stared at the dark thick bars on the wooden counter.

"I guess we ought to chop it up," Lizabeth said.

"Some," Kat agreed, "but we don't have to do that much. It'll all blend in with the cream when we mix it."

Lizabeth found two large serving spoons and a soup ladle. First they took turns mixing. Then they all crowded around the bowl and stirred in unison. They mixed until their arms ached, with big sweeps of the bowl and little ones. Kat tried using her spoon as a beater. So then they beat and mixed. Strangely enough, the contents of the bowl didn't look much like ice cream. Big chunks of ice floated next to chunks of chocolate. The cream took on a brownish hue. It became more liquid as narrow ice shards melted.

Amanda stopped. "Something's wrong."

"I know!" Kat snapped her fingers. "It needs salt! I'm sure I've heard something about salt and freezing."

"Well, let's see." Lizabeth emptied a big salt shaker into the bowl.

They stirred it around and around. The strange brownish color of the cream became somewhat darker.

Kat's face fell. "It's not setting. It's definitely still liquid."

"So it's not ice cream," Lizabeth admitted. "We'll call it an ice cream *drink!*"

Kat brightened. "*Chocolate ice cream drink.* Doesn't that sound good?"

"And then we won't even need to hand out spoons. Only cups," Lizabeth said.

"I think we'd better taste it first," Amanda said.

"Go ahead."

Amanda dipped a spoon into the mix and sipped. She swallowed hard.

"Well, what? What?" the others prompted.

"It's, um, salty."

"Oh. Well, yes. I guess it needs sugar," Kat said.

"Lots of sugar," Amanda added. "The chocolate is bitter!"

Lizabeth poured a one-pound bag of sugar into the bowl. They stirred some more.

"We'd better get it out to the green now," Kat said. "I have to be home in time for my lighthouse watch."

At the village green, the girls set up a card table. They

lined up paper cups around the big bowl and chanted, "I scream, you scream, we all scream for ice cream! A brand-new chocolate ice drink! Come one, come all. Only ten cents a cup!"

A lot of people scurried past through the blustery wind. Mr. Thomas paused for a moment on his way across the lawn.

"Now if you were selling *hot* chocolate on a day like this, I'd be a customer," he said.

"I never thought of that," Amanda mumbled. "It is kind of cold for ice cream."

"Especially ice cream that isn't . . . quite ice cream," Lizabeth added.

"Don't give up, we're just getting started!" Kat insisted. "Come one, come all! A new chocolate ice cream drink! Chocolate all the way from San Francisco! Only ten cents a cup!"

A few people stopped, peered into the bowl, and hastily went on.

"A brand-new chocolate ice cream drink! Only eight cents a cup!" the girls chanted.

And after a while, "Step right up and try our choco-late ice cream drink! Only five cents a cup!"

Mr. Alveira, from the Alveira & Sons Boatyard,

stopped. He smiled at them sympathetically. "Well, if you girls are working so hard, I'll have to try a cup. Here you go." He handed a nickel to Kat. Then, as Lizabeth poured for him, he took a closer look into the bowl. "It looks like, um, exactly what's in that?"

"Only the freshest ingredients, Mr. Alveira," Kat told him. "Fresh dairy cream and chocolate from San Francisco and—"

He hesitated. Three pairs of hopeful eyes were glued to him. Bravely, he raised the paper cup to his lips and took a sip. He sputtered and coughed. Kat was alarmed. Was one of the chocolate chunks stuck in his throat? Or even worse, a shard of ice *piercing* it?

"Are you all right, Mr. Alveira? Nod if you want me to pat your back!"

He caught his breath. "No, thank you," he managed to cough out. He handed the half-full cup back to Kat and cleared his throat. "I'm not . . . very thirsty." He walked away as fast as he could without actually running.

Kat followed him. "Mr. Alveira? Do you want your nickel back?"

"No, that's quite all right, Katherine. . . . Good luck with your, er, concoction."

Kat went back to Amanda and Lizabeth. "I think . . .

I think we'd better stop."

"I vote for pouring the whole thing down the sewer," Lizabeth said.

"Oh, no!" Amanda said. "It's wrong to waste food. I mean, all that cream and chocolate! My father teaches us to respect good food, especially when there are so many needy people."

Kat agreed. "It's sinful to throw it away. Just the cream alone— It should be put to use."

"Well, what do you plan to do with it?" Lizabeth asked. "If you give it to charity, I don't think they'll be grateful."

"We have to drink it ourselves," Kat said.

Amanda nodded.

"Count me out," Lizabeth said. She watched as they drank their first cup. "What does it taste like?"

"Very rich," Kat said.

"And very sweet," Amanda said.

"With a kind of salty thing around the edges," Kat added.

"And very, *very* rich," Amanda repeated. "With lumps."

They each forced down a second cup. It seemed as though they hadn't even made a dent in the brimming bowl.

"You're not going to finish all of it, are you?" Lizabeth asked.

"I'll try." Kat's voice had become very small. "Waste not, want not." She glanced at Amanda. Amanda downed her third cup. Her face looked drawn; her skin had taken on a greenish pallor. Kat suspected she looked the same way.

Kat started another cup. The excess sweetness made her mouth pucker. A lump of bitter chocolate sat in her mouth. "I can't do this," she whispered.

"Me either," Amanda moaned. "I'm . . . I'm sick to my stomach."

Kat and Amanda reeled along Lighthouse Lane to their homes. Kat continued on alone, taking deep shuddery breaths all the way. She skipped dinner that evening. At the sight of the remaining chocolates from the Carstairses, she clapped her hand over her mouth.

It was November ninth and she was exactly one nickel closer to her goal—at the cost of feeling horribly guilty about nice Mr. Alveira. On the bright side, she thought, she was forever cured of her sweet tooth.

ten

fter school the next day, the girls walked along Lighthouse Lane.

"Were you sick last night?" Amanda asked Kat.

"Well . . . not seriously," Kat said.

"Father was upset that I didn't eat dinner," Amanda said.

"Let's please forget about ice cream drinks," Kat said.

"Are we really going to do *yard work* all afternoon?" Lizabeth asked.

"I can't think of anything else right now," Kat said. "You don't have to."

Lizabeth sighed. "I said I'd help, so I will."

"The good thing about raking leaves," Kat said, "is that new ones keep falling. So we'll have lots of repeat customers."

"We'll need dozens of customers to earn twenty dollars," Lizabeth said.

"Twenty dollars minus a nickel," Kat corrected. "I'll have to work every single day." It was already November tenth and December fifteenth wasn't that far off. "Look, that front yard is drowning in leaves! Let's go."

Kat led the way up the front path and rang the doorbell.

Mrs. Peterson opened the door. "Katherine, Amanda, and Lizabeth, my three favorite young ladies. You all looked lovely at the barn dance, all grown up."

"Thank you, Mrs. Peterson," Lizabeth said.

"Mrs. Peterson? We saw the leaves in your yard," Kat said, "and we could rake them up for you. It's only twenty cents for all three of us."

"I don't think so, Katherine."

"Or fifteen cents," Kat pleaded.

"We'd bag them neatly," Amanda said, "and do a clean job for you."

"They do need raking, but it's not a job for girls," Mrs. Peterson said. "I'm sorry, but I'd feel very uncomfortable."

"But Mrs. Peterson—"

Mrs. Peterson shook her head. "It's just not appropriate."

Kat, Amanda, and Lizabeth went from house to house along the lane.

Mr. Whipple looked amazed at the idea. "Girls raking? I don't think so!" He turned to Lizabeth. "I could use some help if your brother Christopher's interested."

"Young Jimmy Hanlon does all my odd jobs." Mrs. Killigrew frowned. "Amanda, does your father know you're doing this?"

Mrs. Lee said, "Young ladies asking for yard work? I never heard of such a thing!"

The three trudged on. At one house, there was a compliment for Lizabeth's new coat. At another, someone sent regards to Kat's mother. But everywhere they went the answer was no.

Mr. Justin turned them down, too, but then he said, "Try Potter's orchard. They had a huge crop this year and they're desperate for more pickers. They might even take on girls."

"Thank you, Mr. Justin!" The bounce was back in Kat's step on her way down his path. "I never thought of that. We can pick apples!"

"Potter's Orchard! That's at least a mile from here," Lizabeth complained.

"One mile isn't that far," Amanda said.

But the mile ran mostly uphill along curving roads. And what made it seem extra far to Kat was having to listen to Lizabeth all along the way. "This is ruining my new shoes," and "I'm not dressed for hiking," and "I'm used to riding in a horse and carriage."

"Lizabeth, we're almost there," Kat said wearily.

They passed farmland with widely spaced houses. They passed by a red barn and a pasture with grazing cows. They passed neat haystacks. Kat was about to jump into one, but no, she had serious business to take care of today.

Kat didn't want to admit it, but by the time they reached Potter's, she was worn out. Amanda said, "I feel like we've done an afternoon's work before we've even worked."

At the orchard, they made their way through long aisles of apple trees. The winey fragrance of ripening apples drifted through the air. They passed groups of men and boys hoisting baskets of apples and climbing up ladders. They found Mr. Potter near the main house.

"Mr. Potter, we heard you need pickers," Amanda said.

"And here we are, all ready to work," Kat added.

"*Girls* picking?" Mr. Potter scratched his white beard. "I don't know about this."

"Please, Mr. Potter," Lizabeth said. "We came a long way."

"We're good workers," Kat said.

"It's a sin to let the apples rot on the trees," Amanda said.

He hesitated and cleared his throat and hesitated some more. Finally he said, "All right. Bushel baskets, ten cents for each full basket."

Kat nodded eagerly.

"Get your baskets from Hiram over there—the tall man in the checked shirt—and bring them back to me when they're full."

"Yes, sir!" Kat said. "Where do we get the ladders?"

"I don't want you on ladders," Mr. Potter said. "Pick whatever you can reach."

"But—but why can't we use ladders?"

"I have daughters of my own and I'm not about to have any girls climbing ladders! If I wasn't so short-handed today . . ." He pointed to the far edge of the orchard. "Start over there, by the fence."

The man named Hiram looked surprised as he gave them baskets.

The fence was far away from any of the other workers. "I guess Mr. Potter doesn't want anyone to see that he hired us," Amanda said.

There weren't many apples on the lowest branches and they had to reach up high to pick even those. Kat's shoulder began to ache from the constant stretching. Amanda stood on tiptoe; her lips were set in a grim line. After a few tries at reaching for the crop, Lizabeth sat down against the trunk of the tree and munched on a McIntosh.

Kat glanced at her. "We'll never get anything done that way."

"We're not getting anything done anyway," Lizabeth answered.

It was true; apples barely covered the bottom of one basket.

"What if I shake the tree?" Kat asked.

"It's too big to shake and if the apples fall, they'll be bruised," Amanda said.

"I know, I'll climb up and hand them down to you," Kat said. She found a toehold and shimmied up to a crotch in the trunk. It had been a lot easier to climb when she was younger, when she could still wear tights and skirts to just below the knee, like Tracy and Hannah. Kat handed a few apples down to Amanda and Lizabeth, but the big crop was still too high to reach. She had nothing to show for her effort but a skinned ankle.

Kat jumped down to the ground. "This doesn't make sense. I need a ladder."

"But Mr. Potter said—" Amanda started.

"You can't climb up a ladder. Your *unmentionables* will show!" Lizabeth said.

"So what? There's no one here but us." Kat looked around the orchard. "I'm going to look for one!"

Kat walked through aisles of trees. The other crews were almost out of sight. Far off in the distance she saw a shed and a boy going toward it, carrying a ladder over his shoulder.

She ran down toward the boy. "Hey! If you're through with it, I want it!"

The boy turned around. His hair was as black as a raven's wing and his eyes were startlingly blue. It was *him*! The boy from the barn dance, Christopher's friend Michael!

"What do you want with a ladder?" he asked. "Wait a minute! You're Lizabeth's friend, aren't you? Is it Cat, as in 'meow'?"

"K-A-T, short for Katherine."

"Oh. Then I can call you Katie."

"You can call me that but I won't answer," Kat said.

"What?"

"That's not my name. I mean, no one calls me Katie. Well . . . I guess you can . . . if you want to. I don't mind if . . . I mean, maybe I'd answer if—" She stopped short; she was babbling like an idiot!

Kat squirmed under his blue-eyed stare. She didn't know what to do with her arms and legs. She had to say *something.* "What are you doing here? I thought you lived in Cranberry."

"How do you know where I live?"

Oh, no. Now he knew she'd been asking about him! She could tell by his big grin. Kat prayed she wouldn't blush.

"Mr. Potter's my uncle. I come here to help out in picking season. What are *you* doing here?"

"Picking," Kat said. "Apples."

"You?" His eyebrows lifted. "No, seriously."

"Yes! What's so strange about that?" All day long people had been telling her what girls shouldn't do. She was sick and tired of it! "And I need the ladder," Kat said.

He took in the long skirt that reached her ankles. "You're planning to climb up in that?"

"Of course I am! What's the problem? It's not my fault if I don't have trousers!" She'd have to hike up her skirt and her petticoat. Lizabeth's warnings came back to her. "But don't look, all right? Promise."

"I promise." He looked confused. "But . . . don't look at what?"

"Oh, never mind!" Kat wanted to kick herself for saying anything. She sure wasn't going to explain! "Please just give me the ladder!"

"You can't carry it by yourself."

"I can so carry it! As well as anybody! Why does everyone think girls are so helpless?"

"Listen, Katie, I'm only trying to act like a gentleman."

"Just put it up on my shoulder!"

Michael laughed. "All right! I'm not about to fight with a prickly redhead." His hand grazed her shoulder to adjust the ladder and Kat was surprised by the shivery feeling that ran up her back.

"I swear, I've never met a girl like you before."

Was that good or terrible, Kat wondered. Just possibly, just maybe, it was good because he said it with such a friendly smile. As if, maybe, he liked her! Wait, was that a nice smile, or was he *laughing* at her? How dare he!

Kat carried the ladder back to Lizabeth and Amanda. *Prickly*, on second thought, definitely wasn't good. Well, she didn't care a bit. Michael was horrible!

She steadied the ladder against the trunk and pulled her skirt up out of the way in spite of Lizabeth's shocked expression. Kat took a cautious look around. Michael was way off in the distance somewhere. She couldn't see the shed through the trees. She climbed up to a big bunch of apples.

The girls fell into a work rhythm. Kat handed apples to Amanda, standing on a lower rung; Amanda gave them to Lizabeth, who placed them in the basket.

They didn't know she'd met Michael, Kat thought. She never kept anything from her friends but there was nothing at all to tell, was there? Except that Michael made her feel bewildered and jangled. Maybe if she saw him again . . . How could she have forgotten? She'd be far away in Boston.

As the afternoon light began to fade, three very tired girls dragged three baskets of apples to Mr. Potter at the main house.

Mr. Potter examined the baskets. "*Almost* full, but not to the top. All right," he said. "I'll give you ten cents for each. Thirty cents."

"Thank you!" Kat said. "We'll come back tomorrow."

"No, I have some other crews coming tomorrow."

"But we did a good job," Kat protested. "We'll start earlier—we'll fill them all the way."

"No. Thank you, girls. You did fine, better than I expected, but this isn't women's work."

If Kat heard that one more time! She glanced at Lizabeth and Amanda; no reaction at all. If "women's work" seemed normal to everyone else—to Ma, even to her best friends—then maybe she was truly odd to object.

On the long walk back to Lighthouse Lane Kat did the arithmetic. "Thirty cents from twenty dollars leaves nineteen dollars and seventy cents. Minus one nickel. . . . Nineteen dollars and sixty-five cents to go." She sighed. "I have nowhere near enough."

"We'll find something else to do," Amanda said.

"Ten cents each," Kat said slowly. "The two of you earned your share. It's really yours, and I don't know if I should—"

"Of course you should," Lizabeth said. "We *want* to help."

"That's what friends are for," Amanda added.

"I spent all my savings on a new parasol," Lizabeth said. "It's aquamarine with the prettiest ruffle. But now I wish I still had the money to give to you."

"I love you both so much!" Kat pulled them into a big bear hug. "I'm so lucky to have such good friends."

As long as she was with Amanda and Lizabeth, Kat didn't feel too discouraged. But when they separated at Lighthouse Lane and Kat walked on to Durham Point by herself, reality washed over her. It was November tenth and she had to allow time for the mail to reach Boston by December fifteenth. She had only four weeks left.

Kat came home from the orchard barely in time for her lighthouse shift. She gobbled down a quick supper and automatically started to reach for an apple from the bowl on the table to take up to the tower with her. Wait, the last thing on earth she wanted was an apple!

Kat settled into her chair and scanned the horizon. The sun was setting and turning the sea into glorious shades of rose and gold. It was a scene begging for her watercolors. The light of the kerosene lantern was too dim for mixing colors, but at least she could sketch. She had read somewhere that the human hand was the hardest thing to draw well. She could use her left hand as a model and sketch with her right. The more she practiced, the better she'd be when she arrived in Boston. *If* she arrived in Boston. No, she wouldn't allow herself to doubt. She *had* to think of something she could do to make money.

Kat crossed to the shelf where she kept her art supplies. She picked up her sketch pad and the Carstairses' letter peeked from between the pages. The letter was grimy and wrinkled from her many rereadings. Next to it was the carefully folded gift paper that had wrapped the box of chocolates. Kat touched it gently.

Suddenly, Kat's eyes widened. Yes, this was it. She had the answer right in front of her nose!

eleven

The gift paper, with its red and blue designs over a shiny gold background, was beautiful. Any gift, even the simplest, would seem special wrapped in paper like that. So different from the plain white paper they had in Cape Light.

Kat examined the paper more closely. The red and blue were curlicued squiggles, pretty, but not hard to imitate. Could she? Of course! She didn't have shiny gold paper like that, but she could paint designs all over a white background, pale blue and lilac snowflakes for winter, red and green bells for Christmas. Or red-striped candy canes, or green pinecones! Winding yellow or pink ribbons for birthdays, red hearts for Valentine's Day, colorful dots for any-occasion gifts. . . . Kat caught her breath as ideas kept coming. This was something she could do and surely the people of Cape Light would want it. Maybe she could sell her gift paper to the general store and the Pelican Street Bookshop! She needed to make samples.

For the rest of the evening, Kat squinted in the light of the lantern and painted designs on the pages of her watercolor tablet. She labored over the pale blue and lilac snowflakes, each one different. She was pleased with the results. Next, she painted scattered red balloons with trailing strings. There was a flutter of excitement in Kat's stomach. This was going well! Oh, she wished she didn't have to keep stopping to scan the horizon! But it was her job and she did it, however impatiently. Yellow stars . . . she redid them; they looked nicer if they weren't too crowded. The bright red hearts were easy. They went fast.

At the end of her shift, Kat nodded with satisfaction. Almost a dozen pages of designs were propped up to dry on the shelf.

The next day, Kat was anxious as she climbed up the ladder to the tower. Would her designs still look as good in daylight? In the tower, she examined them critically. She tore up the green pinecones: the color was muddy and you couldn't tell what they were supposed to be. The stars, well, chrome yellow was too garish; pale yellow would be prettier. She'd redo them. The rest had turned out well, she thought. Kat picked the best samples to show.

On her way to Lighthouse Lane she waved to Papa on the roof of the cottage. He'd been working up there for days.

"Morning, Papa," she called.

"Morning, Kat," he called back. "I saw your pages on my watch last night. Different from the things you usually paint. Nice, though." He moved gingerly from one part of the roof to another. "What are they for?"

Kat hesitated. Her gift paper might go the way of the ice cream drink and the raking project. It would be better to surprise him later, if this worked out. "Just something I'm trying," Kat called back.

At the general store, Mr. Thomas studied the snowflake page. "Hmmmm," he said.

Kat held her breath and crossed her fingers.

"Gift paper, eh?"

"Yes, sir." Kat's mouth was dry. She fidgeted nervously.

"Just the other day Mrs. White was in for the mister's birthday present and she was pining for some fancy wrapping. I'll tell you what, Katherine, I'll try the snowflakes. And the ribbons. And . . . hmmm . . . the dots, too. I'll try a dozen sheets of each. Thirty-five cents a dozen."

"Thank you, Mr. Thomas! But Mr. Thomas, they're hand-painted." There was a sudden catch in Kat's voice. Was she pushing too hard? She'd never done anything like this before!

"Hmmmm. All right, forty cents a dozen, paid on delivery."

"Thank you!" Her first sale! "I'll have them ready for you in no time! I'll need some of your white wrapping paper to paint on."

Mr. Thomas unrolled the spool of wrapping paper behind the counter. "Let's say . . . two feet for each sheet. That should be big enough to wrap most anything."

Kat watched him cut the paper into two-foot sections and place them in a brown paper bag. Forty cents for a dozen sheets, times three. One dollar and twenty cents!

Flushed with success, Kat stopped in at the bakery.

Mr. Witherspoon stood behind the counter in a smock dusted with flour.

"Hello there, Katherine. Was there much storm damage out your way?"

"Some broken shingles on the cottage roof."

"Not too bad, I hope. Well, what'll it be today? I have some nice chocolate cookies still warm from the oven."

"No, thank you, Mr. Witherspoon, I've sort of given up chocolate. I'm here to show you my samples."

"Samples? What kind of samples?"

"For gift wrapping paper." She spread her pages out on the counter. She was less nervous now that she had practiced on Mr. Thomas. "I thought you might want some."

"Nice, but what do I need with wrapping paper? Everything here goes into cardboard boxes."

"Mr. Witherspoon, lots of people bring a box of cookies when they go visiting. If they wrapped the box in pretty paper . . . well, that's more of a gift, isn't it? Or cakes for special occasions?"

"That's not a bad idea." Mr. Witherspoon cleared his throat as he thought. "Those dots . . . They're cheerful, aren't they? And the Christmas bells, though Christmas is still far off."

"It'll be here before you know it," Kat said.

"How much do you want for it?"

"Only forty cents for a dozen sheets. Two-foot sheets."

Mr. Witherspoon frowned.

"Mr. Witherspoon, it's all hand-painted."

"I don't know . . . I don't know . . . Well, all right. I'll see how it goes over with my customers. I'll try the dots and the Christmas bells."

Forty cents times two is eighty cents, Kat thought, plus one dollar and twenty cents from Mr. Thomas. She'd be getting two dollars!

On her way to Pelican Street and the bookshop, Kat hummed a bit of the popular song "Meet Me in St. Louis, Louis" but the words in her mind were "Meet Me in Boston, Boston. . . ."

Mrs. Cornell at the Pelican Street Bookshop didn't hesitate the way Mr. Thomas and Mr. Witherspoon had.

"These are lovely, Katherine—especially the snow-flakes," she said. "Each one is different; you can see immediately that they're handmade. I'll take three dozen of the snowflakes and three dozen of the ribbons. The hearts would be nice for Valentine's Day. Maybe I'll order them later."

"Thank you, Mrs. Cornell. I'll just need some plain wrapping paper to paint on."

Mrs. Cornell unrolled her white paper. "Have you thought of making matching gift cards, too, Katherine?

I'd add twenty-five cents for each set of twelve cards."

"All right! I'll get it all to you by the end of the month."

"That's fine. Katherine, can you make Valentine's cards, beautiful lacey ones with ribbons and trimmings, roses and forget-me-nots, something obviously hand-made? I'd pay fifty cents each for something spectacular. They'd have to be truly special."

"I can do that, Mrs. Cornell." Could she? Kat bit her lip.

"Show me a sample and I'd order in February."

"Mrs. Cornell, I'll get the samples to you fast. If you like them—if you could see your way to ordering them ahead of time—I need to earn a lot before December fif-teenth."

"You have a real talent for design, Katherine. I'm betting they'd be wonderful. All right, if you deliver two sets of heart paper and matching gift cards, and when I see your Valentine card sample I'd order say, twenty-five of those. You may deliver early and I'll keep them in stock."

"Thank you, Mrs. Cornell. Thank you so much!"

Numbers and orders were dancing in Kat's head. She rushed home to write it all down.

Mr. Thomas, general store

1 dz snowflakes	.40
1 dz ribbons	.40
1 dz dots	.40

Mr. Witherspoon, bakery

1 dz dots	.40
1 dz Christmas bells	.40

Mrs. Cornell, bookshop

3 dz snowflakes	1.20
3 dz matching gift cards	.75
3 dz ribbons	1.20
3 dz matching gift cards	.75
2 dz hearts	.80
2 dz matching gift cards	.50
25 Valentine's cards @.50	12.50
Total	$19.70

Kat added it up twice to make sure she wasn't making a mistake. A total of $19.70 plus thirty cents from the orchard, five dollars from Todd, and one nickel: twenty-five dollars and five cents. Even one nickel extra! She'd have to make her deliveries before December fifteenth. Well, by December seventh to allow for the mail. Less than one month to go.

Boston, here I come!

twelve

That afternoon, Kat rushed to the tower and painted snowflakes. The first three sheets were fun. She stretched her arms and back muscles before she started the fourth. And again before the fifth. And the sixth. Kat rolled her shoulders and checked the list of orders. Four dozen sheets of snowflakes. Forty-two more to go!

Ma called her to the cottage for supper. Kat ate quickly, with snowflakes swimming before her eyes.

"You're so quiet tonight," Ma said.

"I'm tired, I guess," Kat answered. Forty-two more plus thirty-six matching gift cards! She ate the chicken potpie in front of her automatically. She still had ribbons, dots, and hearts to do—and Valentine's cards. Getting the orders was the *easy* part!

Kat took a hurricane lamp from the kitchen back to the tower so that along with the kerosene lantern, she would have more light. She diluted cobalt violet with lots of water and a touch of gray for soft lavender snowflakes. She dipped her brush in cerulean blue with just a drop of violet for other snowflakes. Together, the colors were ethereal, until they blurred in front of her eyes. Snowflake after snowflake. Kat put down her brush and stretched. She scanned the horizon. The sea was calm tonight and a full moon floated in a starry sky. How strange it would feel, not being here to see this! But each snowflake was one step closer to Boston. Kat picked up her brush again. She painted until Pa came up for his shift.

"You look tired, Kat. Go on to bed."

"I will. You look tired, too, Pa."

"I've been working up on the roof all day." He sank into a chair. "Good night, kitten."

In her room, Kat moved Sunshine over to the foot of her bed and got under the covers. She fell asleep as soon as her head touched the pillow. She had disturbing dreams of dancing snowflakes pinching and poking her with sharp crystal edges.

After school on Monday, Amanda said, "I'll help you. Tell me how."

"Me, too," Lizabeth added.

They were sitting cross-legged on the floor of the tower, watching Kat paint multicolored dots.

"Thank you, but there's nothing I can think of right now." Kat sighed. "Except for keeping me company." She still had more snowflakes to finish and she hadn't started on the ribbons and Christmas bells yet. "But if you have any bits of lace and red or pink ribbon, for when I start on the Valentine's Day cards . . . the Valentine's cards will be the hardest," Kat said. "And twenty-five of them! How will I ever get them done in time?"

Kat painted the gift paper while Lizabeth and Amanda were there, and continued to paint after they left. She painted every afternoon after school and all during her watch by the light of the lantern and two hurricane lamps. November fourteenth, November fifteenth, November sixteenth. The week went by in a blur of ribbons, snowflakes, dots, Christmas bells.

On November seventeenth, Kat's hand cramped from holding the paintbrush for so long. She soaked her hand in warm water and wriggled her fingers. There, that felt better, but she definitely needed a break!

On November twentieth, Amanda gave Kat an idea. They took a raw potato from the kitchen and cut it in half. Kat carved the shape of a heart into it. Amanda dipped it into red paint and pressed it onto scrap paper. If it worked, Amanda and Lizabeth could do some sheets and it would go so much faster. Kat examined the scrap. No, the hearts' edges didn't come out sharp enough and making every heart an exact duplicate didn't look as good. She had promised hand-painted designs and she had shown samples of her very best work. It wouldn't be fair to deliver any less.

Just when Kat thought she couldn't face one more Christmas bell, a letter came from the Carstairses.

Dear Katherine,

Thank you for your letter. We're delighted that you plan to enroll in the Bartholomew school. We think you'll love it.

The brochure we sent gives you and your parents some basic information, but we thought we'd add some of our impressions.

The school is in Back Bay, one of the nicest residential neighborhoods of Boston. The girls' dormitory is across from the main building on Clarendon Street. There are six girls to a room. The rooms are not luxurious, but they seem spacious. The girls' dining hall downstairs was changed very little when the building was converted from a private townhouse. It has beautiful wood carvings, a huge fireplace, and a crystal chandelier. One evening a week it is the setting of a tea for the girls and a visitor, perhaps one of Boston's many writers or artists. Once a month or so the girls are taken to the Music Hall, the opera, or the theater.

The art studio is on the top floor of the main building, with lots of natural light from the sky-lights. You can use the studio for your own projects when a class is not in session.

We thought you might like to see the school for yourself before you enroll. You're very welcome to stay at our house. Let us know and we'll work out a convenient time for your visit. We're looking forward to seeing you in Boston.

Your friends,

Evelyn and Kenneth Carstairs

Visiting the Carstairses in Boston would be wonderful but what would she use for the fare? She'd write back to them as soon as she finished her job. Maybe she could get more orders. . . .

Skylights in the studio! The Music Hall, the opera . . . Back Bay sounded so—so Bostonian! Kat had a burst of new energy. Bring on the Christmas bells and the hearts!

On November thirtieth, Amanda and Lizabeth raced up to the tower. "Kat! Kat, look at this!"

Amanda's hands were full of small roses and rose-buds made out of pink and red satin ribbon. "What do you think, Kat?"

"They're beautiful!" Kat beamed. "For Valentine's cards?"

"Exactly!"

"You made them yourself, Amanda? How did you—"

"I was over at Lizabeth's and she had lots of ribbons and I just played around with them and twirled them and sewed them in place. Abracadabra—roses!"

"I love them! I couldn't have done anything like that."

"I can make lots more," Amanda said.

"And I brought leftover lace trim," Lizabeth said. "I'm not exactly artistic, but I can paste."

Kat designed the cards. She cut out and painted hearts, Lizabeth pasted lace borders, and Amanda attached roses and rosebuds. "It goes so fast with the three of us," Kat said.

"Like mass production in one of those new factories." Lizabeth laughed.

"They turned out much better than my sample. Thank you!"

❦

By December first, Kat was ready to deliver her gift paper to Mr. Thomas.

On December second, she delivered Mr. Witherspoon's. On December fifth, Kat, Amanda, and Lizabeth put the finishing touches on the last Valentine's Day card. "I think Mrs. Cornell will love these," Kat said. The next day, Amanda and Lizabeth helped her carry everything to the bookstore.

"They're so charming!" Mrs. Cornell said. "With those sweet rosebuds. Even nicer than your sample!"

"I had a lot of help from my friends," Kat said. Amanda and Lizabeth beamed with pride.

On Pelican Street, outside the bookshop, Kat put her hand in her pocket and touched the money from Mrs. Cornell. "So now, altogether, I have twenty-five dollars and five cents! More than I've ever had in my whole life."

"I've never seen anyone work so hard," Amanda said.

Kat's eyes were shining. "I still can't believe I did it!"

"Kat, I can't believe you're really going," Amanda said. "I can't imagine Cape Light without you."

Kat suddenly felt shaky. "I can't believe I'm going either," she whispered. Her dream was becoming reality. She'd actually be leaving her home and her friends!

"The semester doesn't start until January," Kat said,

"so it's still far off." That was enough time to get used to the thought of living in a new place. She'd just keep thinking of how wonderful the Bartholomew School would be. And to have all of Boston outside the door!

"When are you telling your parents?" Lizabeth asked. "Let's go tell them now."

"No, I want to wait until after dinner, when everyone's around the table. Papa will be proud that I could earn this much." Kat's smile became wider and wider. "I think he'll be so surprised and proud!"

That evening, as Kat helped shell the peas for dinner, Ma said, "Katherine, you look like the cat that's swallowed the canary."

Kat couldn't help it. She kept imagining Papa's amazement when she handed him all her money and then his big, happy smile.

~thirteen~

Ma passed the chicken stew around the table. Though it smelled wonderfully of sage and onions, Kat took only a tiny helping. She was much too excited to eat. She'd make her announcement right after dessert.

She listened with half an ear to the conversation flowing around her. Her hand was on the money stuffed in her dress pocket.

"May I go ice-skating after school tomorrow?" Todd asked. "The green flag's up on the pond."

"Are you sure?" Papa said. "Freezing water can . . ."

Kat wriggled in her chair. She couldn't sit still!

"The flag's up, I saw it yesterday and . . ."

Kat was bubbling over. She couldn't hold back for one more minute! "I did it, Papa!" she blurted out. "I did it!" She jumped up and gave him her wad of bills. "Look!" Everyone stared at her, startled. Papa looked at the money in his hand and put it on the table. "What is this?"

"It's half the tuition for the Bartholomew School!"

"Yippee!" Todd shouted.

"Twenty-five dollars, Papa! Half of my tuition!" Where was that big smile she'd expected to see on his face? He looked at Ma across the table.

Kat looked from one to the other. "Well . . . somebody say something! I did it! Aren't you proud? I earned it by—"

"Katherine." Papa's face was drawn. "I didn't think you had a chance in the world of making that much."

Maybe he was just too stunned and surprised, Kat thought; his smile would break out in a second.

"It seemed like a fantasy," Ma said.

"But it's not. It's right here, half the tuition!" Kat stood very straight and proud. "So now we can put it together with your half, Papa. We should mail it to Boston tomorrow."

"That's wonderful, Kat!" Todd said. Why was Todd the only one who looked happy? This wasn't the way it was supposed to be.

"What's happening?" James asked. "What's going on?"

"That's what I want to know." Kat looked at her parents. "What's going on?"

"Kat . . . I don't have my half," Papa said.

Kat blinked. "What? What do you mean?"

"I don't have it."

She stared at her father. "But where is it?"

"The roof," Papa said. "There weren't only broken shingles, there was a big hole and I had to . . . All the money had to go for materials."

"How could you?" Kat wailed.

"The roof was much worse than I thought," Papa said.

"You promised!"

"I don't have the money to give to you. There's nothing I can do."

"But you have to have *something*. The stipend?"

"This family still needs food on the table and the boys need new shoes for winter." Papa's voice sounded scratchy and defeated. He passed his hand over his forehead. "There is no extra money."

"I don't care about food and shoes! It's not right! It's not!" She saw James's and Todd's stunned expressions through a red haze of anger.

"Ma, Kat's not allowed to yell at Papa!" James said.

"I'm sorry, Kat," Papa said. "I wish I could—"

"Sorry? That's not good enough. I *trusted* you!" Kat

knew she was hurting the person she loved most, but she couldn't stop. "You promised!" Blood was pounding in her head. "I worked so hard!"

"I've never broken a promise to you before." Papa's face was ashen. "I never intended to."

"Except for this one! The most important one. The big opportunity of my life and you ruined it!"

"You will *not* speak to your father in that tone!" Ma said.

"The roof was an emergency," Papa's voice had become very low. "It would have leaked and become worse. You're old enough to understand priorities, Katherine."

"You don't know how hard I worked!" Kat's mouth was dry. She was beyond tears. "You just don't know." Her hand shook as she took the money from the table and stuffed it back into her pocket. She couldn't look at her father.

Todd's face was sorrowful. "I feel so bad for you."

Kat couldn't speak.

"Maybe it's all for the best," Ma said. "You belong here, with the people who love you. And what would we do without your help at the lighthouse? I know you're disappointed now, but—"

"Don't tell me it's all for the best!" Kat exploded. She whirled around and ran up the stairs. "Don't tell me that!"

In her room, Kat lay on her bed and stared at the ceiling. She didn't even pet Sunshine, who sniffed at her anxiously. She saw the last of daylight fading away. She could hear the murmur of voices downstairs. No one was calling her for her shift. Someone else could take it. She didn't care.

How could all her hopes suddenly disappear in one horrible moment? Her visions had seemed so real and so right! Walking among the crowds on Commonwealth Avenue, her skirt stirred by the breeze of automobiles passing by. Standing at an easel under skylights, tubes and tubes of paint stacked nearby—all those colors! At the tea in the dining hall, she was wearing Lizabeth's green dress. . . . Back Bay. Beacon Hill.

She couldn't give it up! She wouldn't! If her parents didn't care enough to help her, if her dreams meant so little to them, she'd do it on her own!

She'd talk to the headmaster. She'd offer to work at the school for the rest of the tuition. She could sweep up and wash dishes and make beds. When the headmaster saw how much she'd already earned, wouldn't he let her in anyway? He would! He had to be nice; he was a friend of the Carstairses, wasn't he? She had to go to Boston and talk to him.

The train, the ferry . . . She couldn't use up all her money to get there, she'd need it. By boat . . . That was the answer! By boat! A lot of the fishermen sailed from Cape Light to Boston on Thursdays with the fresh catch. Friday was fish-eating day in the city. She would stow away. On Thursday, the day after tomorrow. Plenty of time to get ready. It was too late to write to the Carstairses—they'd never get the letter in time. They'd said she was welcome. She'd see them when she arrived. She could do this!

After school on Wednesday, Kat told her friends about her plan. Amanda and Lizabeth sat on the front steps of the schoolhouse. Kat saw them exchange glances as they listened.

"Now remember, you promised. You crossed your hearts. You can't tell a soul about this." Kat was too excited to sit.

"We won't," Amanda said. "But Kat, why can't you just write a letter to the headmaster?"

"And see what he says," Lizabeth added. "Instead of going off and—"

"Because talking in person is altogether different," Kat said. "Anyway, I'll be in Boston!"

"You *can't* stow away," Amanda protested.

"Sure I can. Early in the morning, I'll sneak aboard and—"

"You'll be in so much trouble if you get caught!" Amanda said. "A lot of sailors think a woman aboard is bad luck."

"And I bet there are rats in the hold," Lizabeth said.

"Boston's a big city," Amanda said. "You'll get lost."

"No, I won't. I'll have the school's and the Carstairses' address and I can always ask for directions. That's not so hard."

"I heard there are dangerous streets that a girl shouldn't even walk on!" Lizabeth said.

Kat laughed. "Boston was still in the United States the last time I checked. I'm not exploring a foreign jungle."

"Amanda!" Hannah called from the swing in the schoolyard. "When are you walking me home?"

"In a minute!" Amanda turned back to Kat. "You have the nicest parents in the world. Not the least bit strict."

"I know, but they don't understand. They're not helping at all," Kat said. "So it's up to me to make my dreams come true."

"They'll be so upset," Amanda said. "Just because you're mad at them now—"

"I'm not that mad anymore. And I don't want them to worry. I wrote a letter." Kat handed it to Amanda. "Please give it to them on Thursday afternoon, when they expect me home from school. By then, I'll already be safe in Boston. Thursday afternoon, not a minute earlier, or you'll spoil everything. And not a word to anyone. Swear! On our friendship!"

Amanda and Lizabeth nodded unhappily.

"Say it out loud."

"All right, we swear," Lizabeth said slowly.

"On our friendship," Kat prompted.

"On our friendship," Amanda and Lizabeth repeated.

They read what Kat had written.

Dear Ma and Papa,

When you read this, I'll already be in Boston. I'm going to talk to the headmaster of the Bartholomew School in person so that I can go to school there. And I have the Carstairses' address with me and they did write that I'd be welcome at their home. So you see, there's nothing at all to worry about. I love you both, and Todd and James. Please tell Todd to pay extra attention to Sunshine.

I hope the things I do in Boston will make you proud.

> Love,
> Kat

"Kat, this is scary!" Amanda said. "Please, Kat. Let's just go ice-skating after school tomorrow. Please?"

"No. I'm not staying." Kat waited every winter for Mill Pond to finally freeze solid. Everyone would be there, slipping and sliding over the rough ruts in the ice. . . . She shook her head fiercely. "No, I'm going to Boston."

"Well, I won't say good-bye to you, Katherine Williams!" Amanda stood up with her hands on her hips. "I won't! I'm going to pray for you to change your mind."

"My mind is made up," Kat said. "I'm leaving for Boston in the morning and nothing can stop me now!"

fourteen

That evening Kat found her father's duffel bag in the back of the hall closet. Papa used to take it with him when he went to sea. No one would miss it now.

Kat packed her Sunday dress and pinafore, and Lizabeth's green dress. She'd need her very best things for tea and the theater. She chose one shirtwaist and skirt for school. More of her things could be sent to her once she was settled. She packed a flannel nightgown. Kat put in one of her best seascapes, something to show the headmaster that she was talented.

It was hard to leave her art supplies behind, but if Ma or Papa noticed them missing from the tower during their watches tonight, they'd know something was wrong. And there wasn't enough room in the duffel. Anyway, the school would have plenty of supplies and probably better ones, too!

She put the school's brochure and address and the envelope with the Carstairses' address right on top, easy to reach. She tucked the bundle of money on the side. She was all packed up and suddenly she had to swallow hard to get rid of the lump in her throat. She slid the duffel bag under her bed.

Before she went up to the tower for her evening shift, she stopped in the kitchen.

"Ma, I can't walk to school with Todd and James tomorrow morning," Kat said. "I have to leave before they do."

"Oh?" Ma didn't look up from the pan she was scraping.

"I have to go extra early." The boats would leave at dawn.

"Why is that?"

"For a special project. A special school project I'm doing." Kat blushed. She wasn't used to lying and it didn't feel good.

"I'll tell the boys." Ma nodded, without turning around, without asking any questions. Ma didn't have the slightest suspicion and that made Kat feel even more guilty. Kat paused in the doorway for an extra moment, her eyes on Ma's back. She wanted to say something. It was hard to tear herself away but there was nothing she could say without giving away too much.

Kat stood watch for the last time and gazed out at the sea. "Good-bye, Durham Point," she whispered. "Good-bye, Cape Light."

That night, Kat kept waking up to check the clock. At this time tomorrow, she'd be in Boston and starting a new life!

~~~

At dawn, Kat pulled on a heavy sweater, a warm wool skirt, and a knit cap. The hold of a ship would be cold and she'd have to sit in it for hours. She had to decide right now: her heavy, warm everyday coat or the good navy blue princess-style coat she wore to church? The princess coat. She needed her best things for Boston! She added mittens and tied a woolly scarf around her neck.

She hoisted the duffel bag on her shoulder and tip-toed out of her room. Sunshine raised his head but thankfully didn't bark. Ma would have left the tower at first light; she would have dropped off to sleep as soon as she got back into bed. Kat waited, listening. All was quiet. She waited another moment, just to be sure. She went down the stairs, skipping the second one from the bottom that creaked. She opened the front door slowly and inched it shut behind her so it wouldn't slam.

Then she was running along Lighthouse Lane. She hardly felt the weight of the bag. Her excitement propelled her forward and made her fly!

It was good sailing weather, cold and windy but sunny; a cloudless blue sky, nothing at all to keep the boats from heading out. Perfect. The brisk wind reddened Kat's cheeks and shocked her wide awake. She made a right turn off Lighthouse Lane onto the short dirt path of Wharf Way. The docks were spread out in front of her.

Even at this early hour the noise and activity at the docks was amazing. Kat looked in all directions at once. Men and boys were moving back and forth among ships of all sizes. "Hoist it up, come on, this way . . ." There was the sound of grinding chains being pulled by thick ropes. A faint ringing as a buoy stirred in the water. "Let's go, easy does it!"

Pick a boat, Kat thought, quick, before anyone notices me.

Heavy footsteps pounded on the gnarled boards of the dock nearby. "On the starboard side!" someone called out. Several men were leaning back against huge wooden barrels banded with metal; their pipe smoke curled into the air.

Hurry, Kat thought, find a boat. The ones with empty lobster traps and nets being loaded on deck had to be going out for a day's fishing. Her eyes darted to the boats where crates of fish and blocks of ice were being carried below deck, along with squirming, clawing lobsters piled up in huge cages. "Hose them down, Buddy," someone shouted. The catch had to be kept cold and wet to stay fresh for a trip. The night's catch, for delivery to Boston. She'd have to share a dark hold with dead fish and scrabbling lobsters! She could handle it. She could! The trip wouldn't be *that* long.

Kat headed toward the *Mary Lee*, freshly painted and trim. She loitered on the dock next to it but there were too many people nearby. Sneaking aboard would be the hard part! Kat moved over to the *Second Chance*. It was a smaller vessel, but it looked almost new. And they had just finished loading cages of lobster. The men were on deck, adjusting the sails. They had their backs to her. Now, Kat thought. Move fast and be invisible. *Now!* She kept her eyes on the backs of the men, busy, no one turning around; she took a quick step and—

"Hey there, Katherine!"

Kat gasped and jumped a mile at the sound of the voice behind her. Mr. Fiering, a friend of Papa's! One more step and she would have been caught!

Her heart was thumping so hard, she was sure it showed through her coat! It took a moment before she could speak. "Hello, Mr. Fiering." She tried to sound normal.

"What are you up to so early?" he asked.

"A project. For school. About the harbor. A harbor project." That made no sense at all! Kat pressed her shaking lips together to keep them from more nervous babbling.

Luckily, Mr. Fiering was too busy to listen. He was already walking away as he spoke to Kat. "Tell your father hello from me," he said as he boarded the *Second Chance*.

Her heart was still hammering. She had to pull herself together! Kat drew in a long, shaky breath. All right. She needed to get away from the center of activity. And she had to get on board, quick, before they all set sail for Boston!

Kat hurried to the far end of the dock, where there were fewer people around. The *Evangeline*. The berths on both sides of it were empty. She could see the men

taking full crates of fish below. All right. This was it . . .
Go! Then she hesitated. The *Evangeline*'s paint was peel-
ing, it looked old. But she wasn't buying it, just hitching
a ride. She saw Mr. Gardner on deck giving orders. So he
was the captain. She knew him by sight, a heavyset man
with a grizzled beard, one of the regular Cape Light fishermen. Surely none of them would go out on a boat that
wasn't shipshape. Anyway, good maintenance didn't
always show on the outside. Here, at the end of the dock,
was her best chance of getting aboard unseen. And she
was running out of time.

Kat took a look behind her. No one. She checked
the men on the deck of the *Evangeline*. They were busy,
their backs to her, wrestling with a full lobster cage.

All right, now or never. *Go!* She clambered aboard
and dove down the steps into the hold. Oh, no, they were
still loading lobsters! The open hatch let in shafts of
light. They'd see her. Footsteps thundered on the metal
rungs down to the hold. Kat scrambled to a far, dark cor-
ner. She squeezed against a damp crate. In the dim light
she could see men bent over in the cramped space and
intent on the job. If they looked this way . . . A pulse in
her forehead was drumming. No, they couldn't hear that!
They couldn't! Kat didn't move a muscle. She held her

breath and waited. Finally the men went up again. The hatch slammed shut, plunging the hold into darkness.

Kat exhaled and her body went limp. Everything around her was black. Slowly her eyes adjusted. She could just make out some vague shapes. She heard footsteps over her head. She heard awful scrabbling sounds. The lobsters in the cages. Right next to her! Well, she could move over. She started to stand up and banged her head. *Ow!* Her forehead throbbed and she sank down again and found another place to sit. She tried shifting into a comfortable position.

She felt the boat lurch as the anchor was pulled up. Then there was a rocking motion. The boat was just getting under way! It felt like she'd been down here for hours already. There was an awful smell. Fresh fish, Papa always said, had no odor at all. This was a pungent smell of rotting wood and decay. She'd never been seasick in her life . . . but that smell! Don't think of getting sick, think of something else, anything else!

Kat's body swayed with the boat but her arms and legs were tight and tense. She adjusted the duffel bag behind her back and leaned against it. She was trapped in a small, dark space, sailing miles away from her family and friends. What had she done? Stop, don't be a baby. It was only for a few hours. And then she'd be in Boston.

Time dragged by.

So far, excitement had carried Kat forward; she'd been in action. Now she had nothing to do but sit still and think. Was Boston's harbor right in the city or far away on the outskirts? How far was it from the Bartholomew School and the Carstairses' home? Where did you get trolleys and what was the fare? What if the school was closed by the time she arrived and the Carstairses weren't at home? Where would she spend the night? She should have written to the Carstairses and told them she was coming!

The awful smell filled her nose and clung to her clothing. Her legs were cramped. She started to stand up to stretch—no, not straight up! She tried half-stretching, bent over. Sitting again, she pushed her legs out in front of her. She flexed her toes and her feet.

Kat rocked with the boat and had no sense of how long they'd been under way. It seemed like hours. Maybe it *was* hours. She wanted to get up and escape this tight, dark space! She hoped they were at least halfway to Boston.

Maybe it was already afternoon. Amanda and Lizabeth might be skating on Mill Pond this very minute.

She missed them already. And her family—she could imagine their shocked faces when they read her letter. Oh, what had she done? . . . Cape Light, where she knew everyone, where you could always count on neighbors for a kind word or a barn raising . . . She'd never run into that boy Michael again, she'd never find out if he liked her or not. . . .

She listened to the swishing sounds of the waves against the sides. She'd have to wait it out.

Suddenly she heard a different noise, scratchy, coming from another direction. Chills raced up her back. Scratchy noises of little claws against the old wooden boards, coming closer to her. She couldn't see anything in the dark. It's nothing, she told herself, just the men working above me, sounds carrying down from the deck.

Something furry crossed her hand! Kat smothered her scream. A rat? Her whole body jumped in panic. She crawled away frantically, not knowing where she was going. She wanted to escape to the deck! Please, God, she prayed, give me courage.

Kat huddled into a small, miserable ball. Please, God, let us reach Boston soon. Or anywhere.

Her legs were aching and cramped. Her skin crawled. She'd die if something furry touched her again!

She was afraid to move. The scratchy sound had stopped—but was something sitting on its haunches with beady little eyes watching her? Kat shuddered.

She had to stretch again, she just *had* to! Cautiously, she shifted position and moved her legs out from under her. There, that was better. But—her ankles felt wet! She felt around with her hands. There was water at the bottom of the hold! Was that normal? It had been dry before. Stop. This awful trip was making her panic. It had to be normal for some seawater to seep through the boards during the journey. That sounded right. How would she know—she'd never sailed in a hold before.

Now the back of her coat was wet. Oh, her good coat! Water had soaked through to her skirt and petticoat, too! Bent over, she moved to find a dry place to sit. Would a rat be looking for a dry place, too? She didn't want to think about that. She couldn't find a dry place!

Wait! Stop and think. She couldn't see where the water was coming from. Maybe it was just leaking from the fish crates that had been hosed down. That was perfectly possible, wasn't it? She shifted uncertainly. She was damp and cold.

Soon she was sopping wet, up to her knees. Her skirt had become heavy, weighting her down. And her feet were now sloshing in water! Kat shivered. This wasn't from any fish crates. This wasn't normal. But maybe it was. Please, let it be normal. She had to stay put or else she'd be in big trouble. She *couldn't* let them know she was here—or should she?

The water was rising!

Kat heard the hull start creaking and then the terrible sound of water rushing in. . . .

~fifteen~

Kat crawled to the hatch. She couldn't fool herself any longer. The boat was in trouble! She banged and banged on the hatch until it opened. Dripping and frightened, she climbed onto the deck.

"Who— What are you—?" A sailor's jaw dropped with astonishment.

"There's water in the hold! Please! Do something!"

"Wait a minute. Captain Gardner!" he shouted. "Look what we've got here!"

"What is this? What's going on?" The captain came over. The other men gathered around Kat and stared. "Where in blazes did you come from?"

"There's no time to explain!" Kat said desperately. "There's water in the hold! I think something is awfully wrong."

"What are you doing on my boat?" Captain Gardner yelled. Kat shrank under his angry stare. "I don't take kindly to stowaways!"

"Please, sir, listen to me! *Water's rushing in!*"

Captain Gardner still looked furious. "All right. Bud, go down and see what she's talking about. Probably nonsense."

"Hurry, please!" Kat urged.

The man called Bud reappeared from the hatch. His face was drawn. "It's filling up!"

Kat was relieved to see the crew spring into action.

Some of the men rushed down to bail. They immediately returned to the deck. "No use, sir, the boards are giving way!"

"Everyone, life preservers!" Captain Gardner called. The men grabbed bright orange cushioned rings. Some sent up S.O.S. flares.

Kat looked out at the horizon. There were no other boats anywhere. No one to see the flares and no sign of land. Just sea and more sea.

Some of the men worked the sails, turning the boat around, guiding it back to port. "Dear God," one of them moaned. "Let the boards hold."

Let the boards hold, Kat's mind echoed. One thing she knew for sure, if they didn't, no one could last long in the icy sea. She stood alone and terrified, in the midst of the furious activity around her.

The captain beckoned to Kat. He took off his life preserver. "Put it on, fast!"

At first, Kat didn't understand. Then she realized there weren't any extras. One preserver per man, and the captain was handing his to her.

"But . . . it's yours."

"Hurry up, take it! You're young yet."

"I . . . I can't," Kat said.

"Take it! That's an order!" the captain barked.

Shamefaced, Kat put on the life preserver. If she hadn't stowed away, there would have been enough to go around.

"Not that it'll do much good if we have to abandon ship," the captain said.

Kat knew he was thinking of the freezing ocean.

The captain glanced at Kat's stricken face. His voice softened. "If we're lucky, we'll make shore."

But Kat was certain shore was hours away. They were trying to sail the boat back just to have *something* to do.

A man with a telescope shouted, "No ships anywhere in sight, sir."

Suddenly the boat shuddered.

Kat grabbed the railing. "What's that?" she whispered.

Captain Gardner looked grim. The boat shook again. Everyone on the crew stopped moving. There was a long, agonizing moment of silence. Then a splintering sound filled the air. There was a horrible shriek as the wooden boards started coming apart. The boat listed to one side and water swamped the deck.

"Abandon ship!" the captain called.

Another wrenching move by the boat and Kat was flung into the sea. The icy water made her gasp. Though the life preserver was keeping her afloat, every instinct told her to grab onto something.

She kicked her legs. She reached out and hung on to a plank of wood. The boat was sinking fast. She saw some of the men swimming toward whatever parts of the boat were still floating. The captain hugged a piece of wood. Near her, men were calling to God and calling out their wives' names.

Kat watched as the mast, the very last part of the *Evangeline,* disappeared under the water.

The water was frigid. The cold sliced through her body like a million knives. All her life, Kat had heard about Cape Light sailors lost at sea. Now she knew. This terrible, terrible cold.

How long could a person last in cold water? She couldn't remember exactly, only that she'd been surprised by what a very short time Papa had said it was. Oh, Papa!

"Dear God," Kat prayed through chattering teeth. She could no longer feel her legs. "Please help me and all these men and the captain. Please help us come home again."

Her arms went from the pain of freezing to total numbness. She couldn't feel her hands clutching the plank.

"Dear God," Kat whispered. "I want to live. But if I can't, please grant me the strength to accept whatever happens. Please help my family find peace in spite of the grief I've brought them." She stifled a sob; she wanted to be brave.

The words of the Twenty-third Psalm came to Kat and as she recited them, she felt her courage expand and grow. "Though I walk through the valley of the shadow of death, I will fear no evil. . . ."

A sailor clinging to a board nearby heard Kat. He spoke the rest of the words with her. "For Thou art with me; Thy rod and Thy staff, they comfort me. . . ."

Their voices carried over the endless sea.

❦ *sixteen* ❧

urely goodness and mercy shall follow me all the days of my life; and I shall dwell in the house of the Lord for ever."

Kat felt comforted, though the sun that shone down so brilliantly could not warm her. She hoped the sailor who had prayed with her felt that comfort, too.

The sea had swallowed up the *Evangeline* as if she had never been. All that remained of her was scattered debris.

The vast silence that engulfed them was occasionally broken by a snatch of prayer or by hopeless last words.

Kat couldn't feel her body anymore. It wouldn't be long now.

Ma, Papa, Todd, James. All that love. Why hadn't she known, every single day, how lucky she was? Cape Light, Durham Point, Amanda and Lizabeth, barn dances, the tower. . . . She didn't want to say good-bye to it all.

Kat closed her eyes. Her time was coming to an end. She had to give thanks for all she'd been given. If only her parents didn't have to suffer . . .

"Sails!" a hoarse voice shouted.

The cry went up again. "Sails! Coming this way!"

Kat blinked. Her vision was blurry now. There, on the horizon! A boat seemed to be heading toward them as fast as the wind would allow!

Someone was coming for them! With her last bit of strength, Kat looked for the captain. Was that him hanging on to a plank, afloat even without a life preserver? Kat blinked again. The boat came closer, and closer.

Everything seemed to be happening so quickly in a whirlwind of confusion. Kat was in a daze. Voices shouting. So loud. Lines thrown into the water. Sailors hauled up. Arms touching her, tugging at her. It was Papa! Papa, on the *Heron*! She saw him through a fog. Papa's strong arms pulling her out of the sea, his strong arms around her on the deck!

"Papa." Kat's knees buckled under her. What was he doing here? Was she dreaming him while she drifted under the waves?

"My Kat. Thank God," Papa said. He held her up. He pulled off his sweater and put it on her. It came to her knees. Then his jacket, the sleeves dangling far beyond her hands. His knit cap was on her head. Somehow her shoes were gone. A sailor's huge, thick socks were pulled over her feet. She was wrapped tight in a blanket and Papa was rubbing her arms and legs. Rubbing hard. Slowly, the feeling came back into them. With it came sharp twinges of pain. Kat couldn't help whimpering. Tears ran down her cheeks and mixed with the salty taste in her mouth.

"Hold on, kitten," Papa said. "It'll stop hurting soon."

Kat nodded.

"Any better?"

Kat felt herself coming back into focus. Piece by piece, the world tilted back into place.

"You're all right, Kat," Papa said.

Kat fiercely wiped her eyes. "And the others? All the sailors?"

"We picked everyone up. We got them all."

Kat looked around. The rescued men on the *Heron* wore odd bits of spare, dry clothing. She was overjoyed to see Captain Gardner; if he had drowned because of her . . .

The crew of the *Heron* were passing around whatever they had: blankets, sweaters, caps, vests, brandy.
The sun was beating down on the deck and the drenched
sailors tilted their faces up, taking in its rays.

Kat, too, soaked up the sun's warmth.

The boat was heading back to Cape Light. How
wonderful to be going home!

"How did you—how did they know we—"

"We didn't know," Papa said. "We had no idea the
Evangeline was in trouble. We came to intercept you. As
soon as I heard you'd stowed away—Kat, what a foolish
thing to do!"

"I know. I'm sorry. Are you mad, Papa?"

"I sure was. Running off to Boston without a
thought! What gets into you, Kat? If I'd found you at the
docks, you'd have been in big trouble. But I'm too glad to
have you back safe." He smiled at her; his eyes were wet.
"Too glad to be mad at my favorite daughter."

Kat's lips trembled as she tried to smile. "Your *only*
daughter."

"If I had ten others, you'd still be my favorite."

"But how did you know? And on the *Evangeline*?"

"Amanda and Lizabeth came by early this morning;
they skipped school to tell us. Thank heaven for their

good sense! I ran down to the docks and someone remembered seeing you hanging around the *Evangeline*. Captain Caldeira volunteered his boat—lost a day of fishing for it—and we raced to catch you. We tried to follow a logical course, not knowing if we'd find the *Evangeline*. You owe Captain Caldeira and his crew your apologies, and your thanks."

"I know, Papa." Kat took a deep breath. "I have something to say to Captain Gardner, too." He was standing near the railing. Kat walked toward him awkwardly. The blanket was tight around her ankles, forcing her to take tiny, hobbled steps.

Other men were gathered around Captain Gardner. "I knew she needed some work," he said mournfully. "But I was short on cash, and I thought just one more catch, one more delivery. The *Evangeline*'s withstood all kinds of weather . . . and now she's gone. I can't believe she's gone."

A sailor shook his head. "It's a shame. It tears a man up."

"My fault. I shouldn't have taken her out." Captain Gardner drew himself up. "Well, she was only a boat. The important thing is, every one of us is going home again." He looked out to sea, his face full of sadness.

Kat approached him hesitantly. "Captain Gardner? I

want to thank you . . . you gave me your life preserver. And I need to apologize. I'm so sorry I sneaked aboard—I'm so sorry for the trouble I caused. Maybe women on board *are* bad luck, the way they say."

"Nonsense," he said. "You brought us the best of luck."

"But how?" Kat was puzzled.

"You're Tom Williams's girl, are you?"

"Yes, sir. Katherine."

"Well, Katherine, if you hadn't stowed away—if they hadn't come looking for you—there wouldn't have been anyone here to rescue us, would there? But mind you, don't ever do anything like that again!"

"I won't! Never!"

He put out his rough, callused hand and shook hers. "All right, Katherine. Next time we meet, I hope it'll be under better circumstances."

Kat smiled. "I hope so, too, Captain Gardner."

Kat was feeling much better when she came back to Papa. And then she remembered.

"Papa! Your duffel bag! It went down with the boat!"

"You couldn't have fit that much into it—just a few clothes? It was an old bag, nothing to worry about."

"The money, Papa! Twenty-five dollars at the bottom

of the ocean!" She'd worked so hard for it. And that pretty green dress. . . . But I have my life! she thought. I'm going home. Nothing else matters.

꿳

At the cottage, Kat sank into the tub and inhaled the steam. Ma had boiled the biggest pots on the stove for lots of hot water. Kat soaked and soaked. Nothing had ever felt so good! She soaped her hair into a high tower of suds. She scrubbed the salt off her body. She scrubbed off the odor and grime of the hold until her skin was tingling and rosy. Then she put on a heavy sweater and a thick woolen skirt; it was miraculous to feel clean again and truly warm. She ran downstairs to the heartfelt embraces of her family.

Kat looked at them as if a cloudy film had been removed from her eyes. Ma's face, full of love and concern, was so beautiful! James with those soft little-boy cheeks. She wanted to hug and hug him. Her sweet, serious Todd. And Papa. Papa was her rock. They meant everything to her. How she would have missed them!

That evening, Kat insisted on taking her regular watch.

"You don't have to," Papa said. "Not tonight, kitten."

"You want me to take it for you?" Todd asked.

"Don't you need rest?" Ma asked. "If you'd like to go

to bed, I'll bring up cinnamon toast."

"I'm fine, really I am," Kat said. "I couldn't be better! I *want* to do my share at the lighthouse. Tonight and every night."

In the tower, Kat saw her art supplies on their shelf. She gently touched her tubes of paint and the watercolor pad. If she had packed them in the duffel . . . But they were here and not at the bottom of the ocean; they were safe and waiting for her.

I'll keep working on my art, she thought, right here in Cape Light. Someday, she'd get the training she wanted, someday she could still go to Boston or another big city. Later, when her family didn't need her so much at the lighthouse. When she was older and far more ready to leave everyone and everything she loved. In the meantime, she would paint and learn from her mistakes and paint some more. Maybe it's better to keep trying and experimenting on my own for a while, Kat thought, before I depend on someone else to show me how. Maybe I'll develop my own style and the critics will see a fresh new talent. She was dreaming again, Kat knew, but she was going to hold on to her dream. It had changed a little, that's all. It left room for all the good things in her life in Cape Light.

Kat followed her usual routine: climbing up the second ladder to the top of the tower, checking the glass around the light—it was spotless, thanks to Todd—and winding the spring that made the light revolve. Then she climbed down and shoveled coal into the stove. She lit the coals, trimmed the wick of the lantern, and pulled her chair to the window.

The sea glistened in the moonlight. A merciless sea, Kat knew, but she still loved it.

Kat heard footsteps on the lower ladder and then Amanda appeared in the tower.

"Kat?" Amanda said. "Your mother said you were up here." She looked very uncomfortable.

"Hi, Amanda! Wait till I tell you what happened to me!" Kat stopped short, puzzled. "Aren't you out awfully late tonight?"

"I had to come and talk, even if you're mad. Lizabeth was afraid to even face you." Amanda cleared her throat. "Kat, can we still be friends?" She seemed close to tears.

"Of course! Why wouldn't we be?"

"Because . . . I feel so bad, Kat. Lizabeth and I *swore* not to tell, but we were so worried. We didn't know what to do. We *had* to tell someone. We couldn't wait until after school, because if you were in trouble or . . . We were so scared. So we decided, even if you'd never forgive us, we still had to tell your parents right away. I'm sorry, Kat. So is Lizabeth."

"Don't be sorry! You saved my life, that's all! Mine and all the men on board! If you hadn't told . . . I mean, no one would have come after me. They found us just in time!"

"I hope you'll . . . Will you ever trust me again?"

"I'll *always* trust you. With *anything*! I was plain crazy and you did the right thing. When I was in that hold, I started to realize dreaming about Boston was one thing, but actually leaving, well, Cape Light is exactly where I want to be. At least for now. And you're the very best friend I'll ever have."

Amanda beamed. "I'm so glad, Kat!"

"Me, too."

"You worked so hard for that Boston money. What are you going to do with it now? Are you going to—"

"It's at the bottom of the ocean." Kat shrugged at Amanda's shocked look. "It's all right. I owe Todd, and I'll make Valentine's cards and things until I can pay him back. And I discovered that I *can* earn money. That's a good thing to know. I guess I'll keep making gift paper— well, not as much and not as fast—then I can buy more paints and brushes and—"

Kat heard more footsteps on the ladder and then Ma and Papa came into view.

"Your father has something for you," Ma said. Papa was holding a small package covered with her ribbon gift paper. Kat looked at him, puzzled.

"From the Pelican Street Bookshop. Nice paper." He grinned. "Mrs. Cornell told me." Awkwardly, he held out the package to Kat. "Here—open it."

Kat searched her father's face. She'd never seen him look so self-conscious and pleased with himself all at the same time. It felt very strange to be tearing open her own gift paper! Oh, a book. *Masters of Watercolor*! "Papa, thank you!"

"That's all Mrs. Cornell had in stock."

"It's wonderful, thank you!" Kat riffled through the colorful, glossy pages. So many paintings to look at!

"We didn't take your wish for art training that seriously," Papa said. "Not seriously enough."

"We should have listened better. It wasn't just a whim, was it?" Ma said.

"When I saw how much you'd earned," Papa said, "I felt terrible. So I went to the bookshop the next morning. Just a token, to show you that we do believe in your dream, even if we didn't have the money to give you."

"I'm sorry, Papa," Kat said. "I understand about the roof. I never meant to hurt—"

"Let me finish," Papa said. "We decided you should get all the art instruction books you need. *Good* ones. Order them from Mrs. Cornell and we'll pay out of household money somehow."

Ma nodded and smiled at her.

A big lump was suddenly in Kat's throat. "Oh, Ma! Papa!" She hugged them both.

"I bet you'll become a *great* artist!" Amanda said.

"Maybe start off by ordering just a few," Ma said. "Give us a chance to catch up, I don't know how much those books cost . . ."

Kat broke into a huge brilliant smile. "Thank you." Her parents were supporting her dreams now. They understood! That meant more than all the instruction books and tuition in the world.

Out the window, she saw the light sweeping around and around in the dark. To guide wayfarers home, Kat thought. Wayfarers like me. The scene before her was hypnotic and mysterious and Kat's eyes welled up. She had been guided home.